BLUE ANOMALY

Hard Science Fiction

J. K. Bunta

J. K. Bunta
Blue Anomaly

Cover art: "Lightforce" by Psyxis, DeviantArt

Editor: Silvia Kotulicova
Copyeditor: Oren Eades

Copyright © J. K. Bunta 2020, 2024
All rights reserved.

Per aspera ad astra
(Through hardships to the stars)

> Lucius Annaeus Seneca (4 BCE – 65 CE)
> Roman Stoic philosopher, statesman, and dramatist

To my beloved wife Silvia and sons T1 (Timur) and T2 (Tobias).

CONTENTS

Title Page	
I – Alone	1
II – Discovery	9
III – Launch	19
IV – Check	27
V – Alienlone	33
VI – Turn	35
VII – Vicinity	40
VIII – Escape	48
IX – Change	54
X – Seconteen	59
XI – Flashback #1	66
XII – Malfunction	68
XIII – Impulse	72
XIV – Postimpulse	76
XV – Probe	78
XVI – Flashback #2	85
XVII – Rover	88
XVIII – Transformation	94
XIX – Landing	96
XX – Convergence	105

XXI – Conference	109
XXII – Contact	115
XXIII – Desire	124
XXIV – Metastability	132
XXV – Candidate	141
XXVI – Alone (Epilogue)	150
ALTERNATIVE ENDING	153
AltEnd XXV – Back	154
AltEnd XXVI – Migration	157
AltEnd XXVII – Another	161
Appendix A: Scientific Foundations of the Story	166
Appendix B: Additional Scientific Facts	171
About The Author	181

I – ALONE

4D coordinates:
our universe, galaxy,
interstellar ship Eremus,
currently forty light-years from Sol, also known as the Sun, in the direction toward the Sagittarius Arm,
year 2121 in Earth time

Alone. Never before had this feeling penetrated his thoughts so deeply, seizing them with unwavering force, momentarily eclipsing all else—akin to a supernova outshining its galaxy with a flood of photons and neutrinos.

There was no turning back. The bridges were burned. The only thing that made sense now was to look forward.

Yet it only lasted a moment. The feelings of emptiness and loneliness were relative concepts, predominantly emotional. Since early childhood, he had remained impervious to emotional fluctuations, even in challenging situations. The unpleasant sensation swiftly vanished, giving way to rational considerations.

It was no coincidence that he had been chosen as the ideal candidate for this demanding and unique journey.

Yes, he was alone. Profoundly alone. Just as he wanted. He had prepared for this. If one were to label his attitude with a traditional term, "eager anticipation" might fit, though it was questionable whether he would truly identify with such a sentimental description. As a person respecting logic, he couldn't perceive negatively what, after thorough preparation, he had come to view as a source of joy. Furthermore, billions of sentient beings on Earth avidly followed his expedition from a forty-light-year distance. He shouldn't disappoint them, even though they would only learn about it in forty years. At this distance from the home planet, the concepts of space and time became truly relative for him, losing their mutual proportions.

He had undergone an exceptionally strict and demanding selection process, emerging as the chosen candidate from thousands of applicants. It wasn't by chance. Holding doctorates in astrophysics and biochemistry, he had a particularly beneficial, necessary, and relatively rare multidisciplinary expertise for the expedition's objectives. Physically surpassing most peers, his youth belied the ample experience he'd gained researching the asteroid belt. Mining corporations, albeit sometimes reluctantly, faced legal obligations to conduct comprehensive surveys, including chemical analyses, before operations—akin to archaeologists examining terrain beneath a future highway.

Beyond his professional qualifications, he possessed equally crucial personality traits. Since an early age, strong introverted tendencies had manifested within him; he often mentioned that those who knew how to be alone were never truly lonely.

Yet, for reasons he found somewhat elusive, he was not an outsider. On the contrary—in the collectives he occasionally found himself in, he was perceived as a positive, relatively communicative individual (speaking sparingly, but when he did, it was worthwhile) and generally well-liked. He'd never gained a reputation as a black sheep or an awkward eccentric, even though he often felt that way himself. He couldn't pinpoint exactly what had earned him the acceptance of those around him, but he logically concluded that several probable reasons contributed to it.

It seemed they regarded him as intelligent—a notion he occasionally met with amusement, aware of his own shortcomings. They respected his unique interests and encyclopedic knowledge. From his point of view, however, there was nothing truly admirable about voraciously consuming information about the surrounding world. After all, for four hundred million years, sea cucumbers at the ocean's bottom had been doing just that, within their capabilities. He'd never lost the childlike fascination with exploration, always seeking to understand causes and associations—questions such as why plants weren't black, given that black absorbed energy most efficiently, were as vital to him as his next meal.

Additionally, his nonconfrontational communication style likely contributed to his acceptance as well. Avoiding conflict was effortless for him, as he viewed earthly matters as mere insignificant rustlings of leaves, unworthy of discord. Lending his electric car to a roommate, who, despite brilliant manual skills, somehow managed to scratch it? Comparing such an event to elements in the central furnace of stars, burning with temperatures in the billions of degrees, was akin to comparing a breeze created by the flutter of butterfly wings to a tropical cyclone's gust.

As a boy, he often said that Earth was just a speck of dust in the galaxy. One day, he recalculated it and was surprised to find that his analogy was deeply underestimated. In reality, compared to the galaxy, Earth was as minuscule as an atom was to a human, being ten thousand times smaller. Faced with such knowledge, how could he behave differently toward earthly matters than towards the whimsical buzzing of atoms?

He admired certain indigenous societies, often regarded as masters of perspective and objective truth, albeit driven by entirely different motivations. For example, he was fascinated by the Amazonian Pirahã tribe. For the Pirahã, only direct observations and experiences held importance, serving as credible sources of truth. Linguistically, the Pirahã language lacked the ability to express that someone else had seen or experienced something, a peculiarity that deeply captivated him. They assigned little significance to any indirect information. They were astonished at how outsiders could believe in things unseen or unexperienced, and even more so, how they could let such beliefs govern their lives. This indigenous tribe valued a similar principle and concept of a credible source and objective truth as modern scientists and he himself did. Anything unprovable was inconsequential, and anything inconsequential couldn't possibly be a problem.

Nevertheless, he knew that others' perception differed from his own. Once, he'd inadvertently left the remnants of a roasted chicken in the oven, only for his roommate to discover them a week later, to her disgust. It had shocked her and elicited a barrage of indiscriminate reproaches. Of course, he'd apologized, but immediately seized the opportunity to delve with interest into the teeming mass of plump, well-fed fly larvae that wriggled in the meat's remnants. Their ability to survive and reproduce was admirable to him.

He realized that most people didn't share his view of the world; hence, he preferred solitude. Despite this, he managed communication with Earthlings and the necessity of integrating into the social organism surprisingly well. However, this proficiency came at the cost of communication, often draining his energy rather than replenishing it. With a wry smile, he humorously termed this phenomenon "endothermic interaction," drawing upon his beloved chemistry jargon.

In any case, the valuable combination of traits, including emotional stability, determination, and other factors, had destined him for this unique journey.

And now, he truly was here. Physically isolated, yet at the center of humanity's undivided attention. What a paradox he found himself in.

And where precisely was he, then? His thoughts scattered and fluttered in confusion. If he were to accurately describe his current state, he would call it disorientation.

In an attempt to find a solid reference point, he directed his attention to the virtual dashboard. Spartan and devoid of unnecessary blinking indicators, everything on it was dynamic and interactive. Holographic projectors displayed only what he expressed interest in or what, based on the evaluation of the onboard system, required human attention. As he had recently awakened from cryogenic sleep, his vision was still adjusting, taking time to adapt to the sensations of his new environment.

This realization once again reminded him of the limitations his body imposed—protected by an uneconomical excess of metal and other materials, necessitated by his physical fragility, delicateness, and vulnerability in the harshness beyond his home planet. Cosmic radiation menaced his DNA, the environmental temperature had to remain within a narrow range, his body demanded continuous circulation of water and a steady supply of complex nutrients and chemical molecules... No, this was not how he imagined efficient space travel.

To clarify, he deeply admired the human body's biochemical and evolutionary marvels—its remarkable complexity, effective adaptation, and coordination, perfectly suited to Earth's conditions. He took proper care of his specimen —hence his good condition—another reason why he found himself in this specific place and time. Yet he saw physical exercise merely as a means to preserve brain health for as long as possible. The brain was what he valued above all. After all, he wanted to live long enough to witness the realization of as many discoveries as possible. That wouldn't be quite feasible with a dementia-afflicted spongy sphere in his head.

Still, he perceived the human body as a burden and a limiting factor in terms of space travel. He lamented not being born centuries or millennia into the future, when he anticipated the biological body might have evolved into a more durable form, perhaps electromechanical. For this reason, he wasn't an advocate of manned flights; he considered the heavy cans protecting delicate biological frailties inside as an unnecessary wastage of material, fuel, and resources. Sending millions of tiny probes with cameras and other useful sensors was much simpler; they could achieve much higher speeds due to their low weight, powered by the energy at their disposal. To him, manned space exploration was as absurd and impractical as watching a neighbor take out the trash with a tractor—amusing, yet ineffably cumbersome. For the cost of one manned expedition, myriad machines could explore a significantly larger space and in considerably less time. From a rational standpoint, such inefficiency was perplexing.

Nevertheless, he recognized that *Homo sapiens* possessed qualities where automated systems lagged behind—namely, flexibility in decision-making and the capacity to evaluate unpredictable circumstances holistically. Artificial intelligence hadn't yet advanced to a stage where it could be trusted with the demanding and costly tasks ahead. Nothing new under the galaxy's stars.

This rationale helped him reconcile with the need for a compromise: a fully automated spacecraft complemented by a human onboard for potentially sophisticated operations. Only a human could adequately respond to the new circumstances expected in this case more than ever before. For the same reason, representatives of humanity would not be thrilled with the idea that, in a possible encounter with extraterrestrial intelligence, they would be represented by a robot vacuum or a coffee maker. Thus, the crew should consist of a single individual—nothing more.

A multi-member crew would introduce risks from interpersonal dynamics, potential strains in relationships, emotional fluctuations—including mutual or unrequited affections—and the threats of cabin fever and disputes. These risk factors would be absent in a single-member mission, simplifying the selection process without the need to consider various crew members' personality combinations. Simulated and previous shorter real flights had confirmed that conflicts could reduce efficiency or directly jeopardize the fate of missions. When selecting crew members, these aspects could not be reliably predicted. And the risk of human factor failure had to be minimized as much as possible.

Hence, the thorough and comprehensive choice of a suitable candidate was imperative, especially considering it was a one-way trip. The return would entail a significant increase in material and energy requirements, as well as the threat of failure. Moreover, technological limitations in cryonics did not yet allow keeping a person alive during the additional nearly forty years of return. Even a one-way trip exceeded all prior research and experimental tests in cryosleep duration. The likelihood of mission failure needed to be minimized to the utmost; otherwise, it would historically represent an unprecedented waste of taxpayers' funds, overshadowing future space endeavors.

To the astonishment of many, there was no shortage of serious applicants for this project, despite ethical criticisms stemming from its no-return approach. Throughout history, the desire for wealth or the necessity of finding new fertile lands had driven humans to embark on groundbreaking exploratory journeys. This had occurred countless times—people first reached Australia tens of thousands of years ago, and over a thousand years ago, Leif Erikson, as the first European, discovered America in this manner.

Yet there was another motivation: the thirst for knowledge and the exploration of the unknown. For some individuals, this desire outweighed concerns about peril or solitude. And this expedition aimed to deliver knowledge that humanity had not yet encountered—knowledge that some people were willing to do anything for.

The mission's objective was straightforward and unequivocal: to meticulously investigate an unexpected and historically significant discovery that initially shocked the scientific community and soon captured the attention of the broader public.

Astronomers had stumbled upon a star defying all standards.

A star that should not have been observable.

A star whose existence could not be explained by any current theoretical astrophysical models.

And last but not least, a star that, merely forty light-years from the Sun—a stone's throw in galactic terms—had not been detectable until recently, according to regular automated sky observations. The anomalous celestial body showered Earth with its photons, captivating the gazes of telescopes aimed at it from both the surface and orbits, intellectually intriguing the increasingly curious minds of Earth's inhabitants.

"Good morning, Tristan." Suddenly, a sharp new sensation pierced into another of his long-dormant senses, interrupting his train of thought. It felt as if the hammer, stirrup, and anvil bones in his ear had rusted over the long period, rendering the sound transmitted through them creaky and harsh.

"Good mor..." He attempted to respond to the control system, but using his vocal cords was still beyond his current capabilities at this moment. He merely nodded slightly in greeting, assuming the onboard system's cameras and artificial intelligence would interpret this gesture as a nonverbal sign of good disposition.

Despite his efforts, this scarcely steadied his usually unshakable thought processes. He was once again adrift in a turbulent sea of neural activity, his persistent search for solid ground yielding only slow and barely noticeable progress.

Gradually, his scattered thoughts coalesced around the control holopanel. His vision began to clear, his eyes' lens muscles responding more quickly, and the irritation from the panel's photons diminished as the automated systems adjusted the brightness in response to his initial reaction.

A moment of clarity emerged… He began to understand the essence of his current existence.

Blue dwarf—the words flashed across his mind, an unexpected insight.

Yes! Heading toward a blue dwarf! From the chaos of his thoughts, he finally seized the crucial information. Exactly—astronomers had discovered a star, a blue dwarf, some forty light-years from the Sun.

He vividly recalled the moment this information had reached him—an event that not only transformed his life, but also held the potential to change the course of history.

II – DISCOVERY

Earth, year 2060

With limited information at the time, he pondered it. *Blue dwarf, blue dwarf. What is that?*

A holographic message in front of him lit up the room in red, announcing:

Scientists discovered a peculiar star, seeking explanation.

It wasn't typical for news like this to take the spotlight. For many, the starry sky was akin to a decorative ceiling clock—visually pleasing, but of little significance in their busy terrestrial lives, which, in their view, encompassed everything important. In some cases, it simply signaled it was time to unwind on the couch and watch a favorite TV series after a day working or caring for children. Particularly in urban areas, even the Moon often appeared only as a faintly pale figure due to light pollution. The brightest planets, struggling to shine amid the myriad city lights and the glow from aircraft and satellites, consistently faded from view. To the typical *Homo urbanus*, the universe's mysteries, with its worlds, galaxies, and peculiarities hidden behind the night's velvety curtain, seemed light-years from their daily concerns. And yet, suddenly, they were making headlines?

"Did you see that?" Tristan tried to direct his current roommate's attention to the news. They weren't partners, and despite sharing a living space, they didn't maintain an emotional or intimate relationship. They understood each other and respected each other's space without forming a deeper emotional connection. It was a purely pragmatic decision —this financially and organizationally advantageous housing opportunity had presented itself, and they, as students, had seized it without much hesitation. Among free-thinking young people, such situations were not uncommon.

"Do you mean that blue star?" she responded with a soft voice, countering with a question. "Yeah, it's all over the place, you know? Even the tabloids are picking up on it, and the mainstream media loves a bit of fresh news. It's perfect for them—there's some real science behind it, no shady sources, so everyone's getting in on it. Personally, I think even the science folks like showing off a bit, you know? Showing taxpayers where the money's going. It's a win-win; spreading the word is always good. Plus, they might even snag more research grants out of it. It's like everything's falling into place, don't you think?"

She gave him a sideways glance and paused. Despite his logical mindset, he seemed less than agreeable, which puzzled her, given her logical explanation. She had expected some acknowledgment or at least a nod of appreciation, not his baffled look.

"But... a blue dwarf. It's blue, you get that?" he responded, his tone serious rather than appreciative.

"What am I supposed to get from that?" The softness in her voice disappeared, replaced by irritation and an eye roll. "Maybe you forgot not all of us are buried in astrophysics like you? A bit of empathy for us regular folks wouldn't hurt, Mr. Know-it-all!"

As a roommate, he wasn't bad, but at times, he irked her with what she considered communication quirks that contrasted with his intellectual and social abilities. Yet, as was often the case, her tolerance and efforts for amicable coexistence prevailed. After all, he didn't mean any harm, and besides, he seemed unusually off-kilter by his own standards. Therefore, she gathered from her memory all the usable nuggets of knowledge that occasionally spilled out during Tristan's random discussions, and she tried to volley them back at him playfully with a subtle touch of affectation for good measure.

"We've got red, white, and brown dwarfs, right? And our Sun's called a yellow dwarf. So, what's so shocking about a blue one?"

At that moment, instead of Tristan, a commentary from some scientist echoed from the holographic news. The holopanel showed a stereotypical balding man, his face lined with wrinkles, seemingly looking right at them. He was dressed in a slightly crumpled jacket, evidently used rather rarely—perhaps only occasionally at conferences, while the rest of the time, it likely languished in the gloom of a somber wardrobe.

In this case, the holovision broadcast seemed to prioritize seriousness, erudition, and experience over the common drive to capture viewers' attention at all costs, quickly and from the first glance. Or was it, on the contrary, part of a strategy? Visually, the archetypal man did indeed embody the very reason he was there—a scientist *par excellence*.

"The blue dwarf is something exceptional, like a revelation from the future, akin to *Homo sapiens* suddenly appearing in the primeval sea alongside trilobites," the bald gentleman began, his pleasant baritone voice and deliberate pace betraying years of university lecturing. "Blue dwarfs do not currently exist in the universe, and for a straightforward reason: the universe is still too young! Blue dwarfs emerge from red dwarfs, which populate galaxies, but only after many hundreds of billions or even trillions of years!"

The guest anticipated a surprised reaction from the news program's host—an "Oh, really?" perhaps. But he miscalculated. Instead of expressing amazement at the large numbers, the host asked emotionlessly, "And what does that imply for us laypeople, Professor?"

The professor paused, appearing to contemplate how to articulate his thoughts. Eventually, he chose to continue informally with a metaphor. "Given that the universe is barely fourteen billion years old, it's currently impossible for a blue dwarf to have formed. If we were to compare the proportions of human life and stars, red dwarfs today are about as old as a one-month-old baby. What you're seeing," he said, pointing to a spot on the large panel behind the host's desk, where a magnified, slightly blurred bluish dot was displayed, "is, therefore, an anomaly—an 'elderly being' that metaphorically should be only one month old[1]."

The host, feigning interest, observed his gesture with affected attention, yet the scientist remained undisturbed. "Research has not yet found any realistic explanation for the observed fact. It's unlikely that our theories of stellar evolution are mistaken in this matter, although there was, of course, a significant effort among us scientists for skepticism. Furthermore..." He paused for a moment, as if contemplating whether to continue with the given thought. "Furthermore, our instruments detected a satellite around this star—so far, an unidentified planet that exhibits..."

Here, however, he came to a complete halt, leaving the host with a questioning look on his face. "What does it exhibit, Professor?" the host asked after a brief pause, this time with genuine interest. Clearly unimpressed by the scientist's lack of polish, he mused, *Eh, he should've had a short intro ready. Maybe they should've picked someone else...* Yet he maintained his professional smile.

"Um," the scientist began, finding his footing, "our instruments have detected unusual emissions from the planet—emissions that defy our current planetary models."

"So, we have an unusual star with an unusual planet?" the host ventured.

"Exactly. But the anomaly seems to originate not from the planet itself, but from a significantly smaller object."

At that moment, Tristan turned the news off. One might say it was the climax, yet he was so engrossed by the information that external stimuli faded away, his brain activity peaking with intense focus. Despite the guest's improvised presentation, he was genuinely intrigued.

His expression distant, Tristan mechanically finished

his breakfast and opted for an unplanned day off. He was determined to dive into the mysteries of blue dwarfs—a topic that was, until now, uncharted territory for him.

***

The Eremus *spaceship, year 2121*

Hmm, as if waking from cryosleep wasn't jarring enough, now memories distract me too, he thought bitterly. *At least they were real, but they're somewhat... mixed... distorted, as if I immersed myself too much in the situation and its actors. Well, after decades of sleep, the human brain conjures up, adjusts, embellishes, fabricates all sorts of things...*

It was not that the memories were unpleasant; they simply diverted his attention from more pressing matters. However, thoughts were hard to halt, especially when a person was in a complex state after the slowdown and subsequent acceleration of biochemical processes.

Thus, he embraced this flurry of thoughts, an involuntary smile crossing his face as he remembered a moment that had forever altered his life's course. Little did he know that such seemingly banal and innocent empathetic insight into the moods and thoughts of others would soon play anything but a banal and innocent role.

"The recovery phase of biochemical processes is complete," announced a pleasant female voice, sounding remarkably natural and offering a welcome interruption to his thoughts. He found it amusing that the designers had opted for such an acoustic expression for the onboard system. There were, of course, countless alternatives, including male ones. Likely, psychologists had recommended this approach, assuming most would find a voice of the opposite sex more comforting—though, given his asexual nature, he found it paradoxical.

He'd always regarded reproduction-related hormones as natural chemical drugs that bound and influenced human behavior, even if it was not always entirely in line with one's will or desire. He was convinced that evolution had created them to ensure the successful reproduction of living organisms—an important but, with a bit of effort, fully rationally manageable task. Modern humans didn't need instincts to avoid extinction. Binding oneself to another individual, often swayed by hormonal drives toward physical attraction, pondering over personality compatibility—what was the point?

Grateful to nature for not squandering the relevant hormones in his case, he handled this aspect of life in his own way—choosing not to waste a significant portion of his existence searching for a partner or succumbing to unnecessary emotional excess, including those evoked by oxytocin and other related hormonal molecules, i.e., love, however positively perceived. Opting for a more pragmatic route, he'd deposited his genetic material in a sperm bank, seeing it as a sufficient contribution to future generations and the propagation of his genes. It was pragmatically simple, materially efficient, and timesaving. With his biochemistry characterized by low testosterone levels, suppressing residual sexual tension was relatively straightforward for him.

Some people pitied him, citing an impoverishment of life experiences, selfishness, or indifference towards raising offspring. This attitude even irritated or aroused suspicion in others, suggesting he suffered from a kind of sociopathy, hormonal disorder, self-aggrandizement, or inferiority complex when seeking a partner. However, he never took their remarks seriously, nor did he hold it against them. He allowed time and sarcastic remarks to flow past like the muddy waters of the Ganges during the monsoon.

He believed the yoke of reproduction turned people into irrationally delusional lovers, intoxicated by hormones, diligently and with extreme motivation working on creation of a predisposition for later disappointment in the case of reciprocated love. And in the case of unrequited love, it was even worse—people became emotional zombies desperately yearning for the object of their affections, not unlike the remnants of the dead that Hindus released into the aforesaid Ganges.

In the end, however, his stance evolved into an advantage, another argument for why he was chosen. Without commitments, or the pursuit thereof, he faced a minimal risk of suffering from separation.

"Basic report, please," he began, slowly returning to normal and focusing on essential matters.

Elektra. I'll call her Elektra, he mused silently, a thought that sprang up unexpectedly and hinted, albeit reluctantly, that regaining normalcy wouldn't be instantaneous. He was not accustomed to making ad-hoc decisions without thorough prior analysis, especially when they appeared essentially unnecessary.

Yet his current predicament seemed to justify the abrupt choice. Waking up after so many years warranted some leeway. The name Elektra itself, logically fitting for an AI rooted in electronic circuits, served as excuse enough—even though psychologists might delve deeper. They could seek associations with Tristan's knowledge of Greek mythology, where Elektra murdered her own mother and her lover, hinting at deeper meanings behind his selection.

However, a more likely explanation—if there was any need for an explanation at all—was simply that the name evoked one of the elementary particles for him. It was associated with the realm where he felt at home, safe, where he had solid ground beneath his feet.

"Date: December twenty-eighth, 2099, ship time. Crew life functions: stabilized. Integrity of the ship and systems: correct. Distance to the destination: 0.221 astronomical units. Relative velocity: 0.0008 times the speed of light…"

"And the date in Earth time, Elektra?" he interjected, breaking the steady stream of data with a question that carried a hint of amusement from using the creative name, half-expecting it to perplex her momentarily.

"Can you clarify the term 'Elektra?'" the ship's system responded, aligning perfectly with Tristan's anticipations.

"I will call you that. Your voice, for some reason, evokes

the name Elektra for me."

A human might take a second or two to ponder a reaction, but for the ship's system, milliseconds were sufficient for such a process.

"Although I have a different designation from my creators, I appreciate creativity. Considering that real biological individuals and literary and mythological heroes bear this name, as artificial intelligence, I regard it as an honor. Thank you," the system said, politely accepting its freshly bestowed name.

He revisited his initial inquiry, steering the conversation back on course. "So, the date in Earth time?"

Elektra replied precisely this time. "December seventeenth, 2121."

Just as expected, he mused. Though not through warp drive—a technology he'd long wished to witness a millennium hence—primitive travel still beat the alternative of Earth's bounds due to technological limitations. The progress in travel speed was not such that ships sent later would arrive at the destination before their predecessors. This could have deprived earlier expeditions of motivation. However, it was not the case in this situation.

The sub-light speed expedition had indeed taken place, and now he sat—or, more precisely, hovered—in space, while Earth, as he knew it, had progressed fifty-six years ahead in time. His classmates, colleagues, and acquaintances were now, at best, elderly; at worst, recycled nutrients savored by bacteria, fungi, and single-celled organisms. He was aware of this fact, but it didn't particularly trouble him. He'd left no family behind; his parents had perished in an oxygen tank explosion at a lunar base when he was still quite young, and he'd never developed an emotional bond with his adoptive caregivers. Therefore, the exact date on his home planet was merely a numerical curiosity for him—an abstract number without a sense of personal connection or involvement. In a way, it provided him with an uplifting sense of freedom, independence, emotional unburdening, and complete liberty.

"How much time until reaching the target orbit?" he asked with a progressively clearer voice, referring to the unexplored celestial body emitting the signals.

"Seventy hours, thirty-seven minutes, fifteen seconds."

Excellent. Though not yet fully stabilized, he felt increasingly active and refreshed—a testament to the biomedical unit's cocktail of chemicals and nutrients administered before and after his awakening. *Excellent*, he thought once again. He was truly looking forward to what would follow—and this time, he might even identify with the concept himself.

His pupils contracted as he observed the bright crescent of the rocky, parched planet through the ship's viewport, where photons bent their paths slightly, giving rise to hues reminiscent of those in Newton's prism. Despite the gray monotony of the planetary surface, these interactions spawned impressive spectrums and intense arcs, which, thanks to the ship's movement, smoothly transitioned in their shapes and geometric arrangements. The result was sparkling patterns, not unlike the beauty of diamonds in the display case of a jewelry store or museum, bathed in bright, elegantly, precisely adjusted, and ingeniously placed lighting. The luminous glow of the still-subtle body no longer required photons to travel distances of tens of light-years to reach him, as they had to for other Earthlings, but a mere several light-minutes.

He couldn't appreciate the artistic beauty of that unique moment. Art had always eluded him since childhood. He considered all paintings and artworks as unnecessary expressions of vulnerable, unstable souls, incomprehensibly serving for others to experience the artist's emotions (as if they didn't have enough of their own). In his view, the closer an image approached to reality, the more beautiful it was. Thus, in the age of photography, he deemed portraits created by people as inexplicably pointless, akin to carrying wood to the forest.

The only exception he was willing to make was for

prehistoric abstract cave paintings, yet only for the oldest known records, such as those in the South African Blombos Cave and the Spanish Cueva del Castillo, as they represented the first known manifestations of the birth of human cognitive abilities, laying the foundation for later science.

However, he appreciated the beauty of the physical processes revealed by the scene. The rainbow colors caused by the varied paths of photons with different energies, influenced by the refractive index of the viewport glass—that was something he found logically and fascinatingly consistent and marvelously fitting within the natural laws of the majestic universe. He felt an integral part of this cosmos, unabashedly immersed in a sea of particles, absorbing the deluge of information, wavelengths, and energy with his eyes...

A quiet interplay of hints, he mused, observing the faint structures in the planet's sparse atmosphere serenely and smoothly hovering in space before him, reaching the peak of his emotional repertoire. From the perspective of an ordinary person in this situation, it was an almost stoic and composed reaction, but for him, it was a remarkable moment.

However, it was not just for him.

And by no means was it the last one...

III – LAUNCH

Earth, year 2064

Boom!

A sudden bang sliced through the fresh morning air. While not exactly an explosion, it matched one in magnitude, intensity, and decibels. Fortunately, at an altitude of almost six thousand meters above sea level, amidst the sparsely populated Himalayan mountain range, there was no one to disturb, aside from perhaps a rarely encountered snow leopard.

The exception was a small group of people standing tensely on a special platform positioned at a safe distance from the source of the sound.

"Whoa, that seriously boomed," remarked a young man with short blond hair, his eyes fixed on the swiftly distancing object, which turned into a tiny dot within a few seconds.

"Uhm." The older black-haired man next to him nodded, evidently slightly shaken by what he had witnessed. "Torben, I didn't expect the aerodynamic boom to pack such a punch from this distance," he continued slowly.

"Henry, they've got it all figured out. Eardrums still holding up, huh? Crazy how fast it vanished…." Torben jabbed his finger into the air, pointing to the empty space in the sky where a quickly dissipating, inconspicuous contrail was heading in the high-altitude wind.

"Yep, just like a legit lightning bolt," Henry observed.

Torben, in the cold, howling wind, pulled his warm protective hat more firmly over his head. Despite his Nordic roots accustomed to harsh winters, the strong air current at minus-twenty degrees Celsius was unpleasant even for him.

Physical limitations couldn't be erased with a wave of a magic wand.

But being here was definitely worth it. Witnessing an electromagnetically accelerated ship's launch wasn't something many outside the space industry experienced. Even for employees within the sector, today was not an ordinary day —although similar launches happened daily, this one was exceptional. The first in a series of cargo ships had just left the Earth's surface, gradually carrying the materials and components needed to complete the *Eremus*, the most sophisticated human-made spacecraft to date. Its challenging task was to transport a selected individual to a strange star with an even stranger satellite orbiting it.

Torben found the name of the ship, set for interstellar launch next year, unappealing. It seemed to him that a rather melancholic individual, or someone betting on the public's lack of Latin knowledge, had named it. After all, who would choose *Desert* or *Solitude* over standard names like *Explorer*, *Voyager*, *Curiosity*, or *Pioneer*? Yes, it was undoubtedly extremely descriptive, but almost certainly chosen with emphasis on the phonetic aspect. They might as well have gone with names like *Depression* or *One-Way*. In any case, from his perspective, this was perhaps the ship's only minor drawback.

The high altitude was essential for the launch. The 130-kilometer-long vacuum tunnel had to open into an environment with the lowest possible air pressure and density. Within the tunnel, the cargo was electromagnetically accelerated to just above Earth's escape velocity. To reduce costs and avoid the need for towering structures, the tunnel's opening was located in a mountain massif. This significantly minimized aerodynamic friction and subsequent deceleration of the ship, which had no onboard propulsion, since it gained the required energy and speed in the tunnel. Small correction thrusters were sufficient for orbital maneuvers. The absence of massive propulsion directly on the projectile was appreciated by space agencies and sponsors, making this method of transportation to orbit extremely cost-effective and, simultaneously, high-capacity.

The streamlined launch process enabled the daily launch of multiple vessels. The tunnel exit only opened for a few brief seconds before the ship passed through, protected from the atmosphere's attempt to rush inside by a high-voltage plasma window similar to what had been used for particle accelerators for almost a century, but larger.

The acceleration overload significantly exceeded the safety limit for humans, but for standard cargo, it was an acceptable and safe value—an ideal way to place components and modules into orbit to complete the first crewed interstellar spacecraft[2].

"How long's it gonna take them to put all of that together, you think?" Henry interrupted the moment of silence after the launch.

"Few launches a day to get everything up there," Torben responded promptly, "and they gotta launch dozens of these babies. That twenty-ton payload limit keeps them busy."

"Dozens? Phew..." Henry turned to Torben with a surprised expression. Although he was here, right at the launch site, he didn't have nearly as many details about the project as Torben. He was just a lay viewer. He had gotten an invitation to observe the launch because it was intended for the motivated lay public, but also thanks to Torben's intervention as a former colleague of Tristan.

For Torben, however, it was a life event, and he couldn't even sleep for the past few days before coming here.

"Just think—it's gonna fly for tens of light-years, and you know, not a robot on board, but a human. Gotta shield him from radiation, sort energy, supplies, atmosphere, and keep all those biological functions running, plus deal with recyclers and whatnot to keep him alive." He emphasized each item, assembling familiar facts into the right picture. "Maybe you read, this miracle won't lug any fuel, like, at all. Few hundred tons for such a task? Pff, easy-peasy."

"Wait up," Henry interjected with a puzzled expression

and a skeptical look, his feathers in the cold wind becoming increasingly ruffled, despite his quality clothing. "How's it without fuel? Are you messing with me?"

"Come on, nope. I'll spill the beans about that trick, but... man, it's freezing. Let's get outta here."

The decision to warm up was apparently also reached by other members of the small group, who had the privileged opportunity to be direct witnesses of a historic moment at an otherwise-isolated tunnel exit. After all, the launch was over, and the condensation trail had dispersed in the dynamic atmosphere, so there was no reason to linger outside and undergo natural cryotherapy.

They first took refuge from the biting cold in the minibus cabin, and five minutes later, they were sitting in the warmth and pleasantly subdued lighting of the café where launch complex employees typically gathered.

"Yeah, but keep it simple. You know I'm not a physicist," Henry suggested.

"I'll do my best." Torben accepted the challenge with a smile. "It all kicked off when scientists realized the vacuum in our universe isn't just an empty void."

"Yeah, caught wind of that—those Buddhist chats about emptiness being fullness and all those quirky ideas, right?"

"Buddhists can say whatever, but in physics, it's a done deal, thanks to Heisenberg's uncertainty principle," Torben continued. However, noticing Henry's perplexed expression caused by an unfamiliar term, he immediately added, "Alright, check this out: for particles, it's as basic as gravity is for us—drop something, it falls. Here in the quantum world, nature borrows energy from the vacuum, 'cause vacuum ain't really empty. Crazy, huh? It's a quantum law. And particles are just chunks of energy. And there are also chunks of borrowed energy, these cool fellas called virtual particles. They pop up in pairs, doing their dance in the quantum scene. But, you know, not for long—that's the law."

Henry managed to follow the thread. "Hmm, sounds like

a wild ride, but fine. But then they gotta be returned, right? I mean, those borrowed fellas."

"Yep, they've got to go back to their cosmic hideout pronto. Like rockstars—here today, gone tomorrow. But, you know, there are a few exceptions."

"Bring them on. I'm curious."

"Alright, buckle up. So, picture this—a strong gravitational field near a black hole. One virtual particle gets greedy, steals energy from its buddy, and bam! The unlucky one plunges into the black hole, while the lucky survivor becomes a real particle with the stolen energy, living its best life. It's like a cosmic drama with a plot twist."

"Huh, sounds crazy, but since up there"—Henry vaguely circled his finger towards the ceiling of the café—"is where the magic will happen, I guess they've tinkered with that a million times. Those Einstein folks pulled off their tricks in labs and accelerators. But seriously, it's kinda mind-boggling. How does it not break the laws of nature?"

"So, no laws would be violated," said Torben, "because the particle that pops up and zooms away from the black hole nabs the energy from its counterpart that got swallowed. Plus, the black hole loses energy, and its mass drops, so our trusty laws of energy and mass conservation stay rock-solid."

"Wait, so the black hole shrinks? If it keeps sucking in those poor particles over and over, it gradually gets smaller?"

"Yep, you got it right on the money," Torben replied.

Though it was a well-known fact to every science enthusiast, Henry was an outsider, merely a friend of a scientist. After nodding in agreement, he sipped his tea, saying, "Well, cool. Keep going; I'm catching on, kinda."

Torben continued with the enthusiasm of someone genuinely passionate about the subject, taking a moment to evaluate his friend's facial expression. "Bringing those virtual particles to life isn't just a black hole game. Picture a tight gap between two surfaces, like a narrow slit. If you move those walls near the speed of light, that's when the particle party kicks off."

He straightened both palms vertically, moving them horizontally towards each other as fast as he could with outstretched fingers, aiming to demonstrate roughly how it worked. He repeatedly separated and brought them back together. Due to the biological limits of muscles, he didn't quite succeed, so the result resembled more the applause of an enthusiastic spectator after a theatrical performance. After such effort, his hands protested against this biologically unjustified movement, and he eventually abandoned his attempt.

In the end, it seemed that the description of the movement of the walls was understood, though not fully embraced.

"Yeah, that sounds insane. You'd need materials tougher than any superhero to withstand those vibrations. I bet even diamond would give up at speeds close to light," Henry said skeptically.

"Exactly. Any regular device would be toast, but scientists? They're clever—always have another trick up their sleeve."

"Seriously?" Henry scoffed, blowing steam off his tea and sipping cautiously. "Don't keep me hanging; spill the beans already."

"Instead of using actual solid walls, imagine they've got these invisible ones, kinda like force fields, made out of zapping electromagnetic fields. Picture it sorta like... an electric vibrator..." Realizing the slip, Torben quickly amended his statement. "Ah, scratch that—think more like an electric oscillator, right? These aren't your regular walls; they're more like waves of energy that dance around. Zap up the juice, and these energy walls start buzzing, creating this wild playground for virtual particles to pop into existence inside the oscillator."

"Uff, this virtual wall thing... I'm lost. How's that even related to propulsion?" With a puzzled expression, Henry blew the steam from the unusually slow-cooling beverage again. Could it be caused by lower air pressure at these altitudes? Either way, he was starting to feel an uncomfortable sense that if he didn't grasp the key to the punchline soon, he might not get there at all, and would feel like a Neanderthal being explained the principles of a hunting rifle.

Fortunately, Torben sensed his hesitation and continued, "We're getting there. As we crank up the speed of the oscillator near light speed, those virtual particles inside start to split up since the walls move too fast for them to team up. Simply separate 'em from each other before they can merge and poof back into void. It creates a scenario similar to a black hole, but here, it's electrical walls and energy doing the pulling[3]. Cool stuff, right?"

"Hold up, hold up. I'm starting to wrap my head around it," Henry said, feeling a spark of understanding. "So, the oscillator pulls out particles from vacuum, they shoot them out of the nozzle, and we've got ourselves some vacuum fuel, right?"

"Yep. Sounds pretty straightforward now, doesn't it?"

"Sounds like some hocus-pocus out of a fairytale," Henry countered with a laugh.

"I promise, no fairytales here." Torben grinned. "It's all legit. Once you generate matter this way, you've got your propellant. Eject it with a magnetic field, and there's your acceleration—no need to haul fuel. Kinda like how a nuclear-powered ship cruises the ocean for years on end using just a reactor and seawater."

"Okay, water's dense, but these vacuum particles... Are they enough? Seems like a lot of energy to produce them, only to shoot out a few..."

"Exactly. So, think of it like those ancient steam engines—kinda clunky and not super slick. It was more of a 'Hey, look what we can do' kind of thing than something you'd actually wanna use. But then, the science wizards got to work, tweaking and tuning. They started with making heavier particles, like electrons, which was a game-changer in efficiency. And then, they went big, bringing in protons, which are, like, way heavier. We're talking serious heft here. Suddenly, these particles were beefy enough to make a difference. Imagine that, over the long haul, this could push a spaceship to almost light speed, and all without needing to haul standard fuel. Pretty wild, huh?"

"Ah, crazy! There's probably a Nobel Prize somewhere in the mix for this mind-blowing stuff," Henry replied, sharing the excitement of scientific breakthroughs. With a sense of joy that he had at least scratched the surface of understanding a bit more about the mystery of the propulsion system for the new ship, he took another sip of tea.

"Exactly! No doubt about it!"

Interstellar flights had already been successfully realized, though without a human crew yet, all thanks to this phenomenon. Indeed, the Nobel Prize had been awarded for it, but not to its original theorist, who passed away before seeing his predictions experimentally verified and advanced.

"Even so," Henry mused, "creating heavier particles must require more energy, right?"

"Ah, that leads us to another big find," Torben said, preparing for another dive into explanation.

"Whoa, hold up, Torby... My head's spinning—could be the thin mountain air or this brainy chat. This isn't like rehashing last night's football match. Let's hit pause and save this for another day. I'd rather not have my brain explode, giving everyone here an unexpected show," Henry joked, chuckling, then took a deep breath and looked out at the towering mountains visible through the cafe's glass atrium, letting himself be caught up in the significance of the moment—a new chapter for humankind.

IV – CHECK

Eremus *spaceship, year 2121*

Not only did onboard sensors confirm Tristan's biochemical processes were fully functional without apparent initial defects, but his own sensations and bodily responses also suggested he had handled the awakening well, dispelling—at least for now—the concerns of the more skeptical doctors.

Every few minutes, strange, deep sounds—reminiscent of an alien poised to burst from his abdomen—resonated from within. However, these were merely signs that his peristalsis was beginning to function smoothly.

Following the initial procedures and biochecks, a more detailed inspection of the ship itself was on the agenda. Despite the vessel being fully automatic and undergoing sophisticated checks throughout the entire flight, a human could still uncover issues that automated systems, even with the assistance of artificial intelligence, might not successfully detect. This was particularly crucial given the duration of the flight, spanning almost thirty-five years of ship time. Yes, it was the frustrating advantage of a holistic approach once again.

After reviewing life support systems (he was alive, so no surprising findings there) and assessing supplies and resources (he was pleased to find that he likely had a long time to live), he decided he was sufficiently prepared for a brief inspection of the ship's sectors. Manual checks were part of the protocol, and he welcomed them as both physical activity and a way to revitalize his body.

He left the rotating section, which had provided his hibernating body with Earth-like gravity through its circular motion in a standard and proven manner over the years. While the spacecraft's propulsion was the latest achievement of science and technology, it only provided acceleration equivalent to one-tenth of Earth's gravitational acceleration, which was insufficient for human needs. Prolonged near-weightlessness would significantly weaken the immune system and other functions of the human body. Moreover, even now, in the active part of his stay, artificial gravity greatly aided him in his movement and work.

He moved to the transition sector, through which he entered the central part of the otherwise-elongated vessel. As he gradually moved from the periphery to the center of rotation, the centrifugal force weakened, causing a slight rise in his stomach. For a moment, he doubted whether exposing his body to such a test at this early stage was the right decision. However, within seconds, his circulatory system adjusted, his blood pressure stabilized, and both the dizziness and the unpleasant sensation in his stomach faded. He felt relieved he wouldn't inadvertently become a cosmic Picasso, splattering the interior with the hydrochloric acid from his stomach. Instead, he could focus on his current goal, the most exciting part of the ship—the propulsion sector.

Despite his rational disposition, contemplating it always filled him with boundless admiration and a profound sense of harmony with the universe's laws. He didn't perceive scientific development as a struggle between humans and nature. While many viewed technological advancements as a victory, a step toward subduing nature, he'd never identified with such an attitude. It seemed foolishly barbaric and primitively regressive to him. On the contrary, as a scientifically oriented individual, he appreciated every piece of knowledge acquired by mankind, shedding a little light on the vast white map slowly and persistently marked with expanding our understanding. He viewed it as a precious gift, a beacon piercing the darkness. And that was precisely how he perceived this amazing invention, the product of the most brilliant minds that had ever set foot on the surfaces of the planets in the solar system.

He slipped into his protective suit with a sense of respect for the complexity of nature and, at the same time, with pride that humanity had managed to understand and harness its intricacy for further exploration. He smoothly entered the propulsion unit sector. Considering the role it played and the speed it provided to the ship, it was surprisingly subtle. It consisted of several dozen massive panels, but he couldn't see them, as they were concealed behind a thick shielding section. He focused on the sensors monitoring the supply of energy to the propulsion thrusters.

"Frequency?" he said into the space, which, despite its role in the vessel, seemed unremarkable in size, visual complexity, or the design of its technology. It was simply, from a layman's perspective, too... straightforward, too monotonous, and too trivially uncomplicated. Yet he had always admired minimalism, understanding that the true challenge lay not in making complex things complicated, but in rendering them simple.

"One hundred and twenty terahertz." It was the expected response from the control system—or, more precisely, Elektra, as he had named it.

"All right. Show me a list of faults that occurred since the beginning of the journey."

A short list of items materialized in the space in front of him, and he glanced over it for a moment. "Our designers and technicians did an excellent job," he continued, nodding approvingly as he scanned through the records. "This is what I call a flawless operation. Even the few minor issues were brilliantly managed by the automation. Hats off to them! Building something this sophisticated in five years... Really, my respect."

A living colleague might have responded to such praise with a joyful nod and a bright smile, but such reactions were, understandably, not to be expected from the central control system.

"And what is this?" He focused his attention on a small red-highlighted record that suddenly appeared on the panel.

"Displaying details now," Elektra responded promptly. "There was a temporary outage in one of the particle generators. It was automatically disconnected when the frequency and energy at its input increased, and—"

"Began generating unstable particles?" he concluded thoughtfully in her stead, continuing his examination of the record.

"Yes," she replied tersely.

Interesting, Tristan mused silently. The creation of unstable particles was logical with increased power. With sufficient energy, particles even heavier than protons could be generated. From a propulsion perspective, this was beneficial, as it made it even more efficient.

However, it wasn't ideal for maintaining life on board. Too-massive particles meant increased radiation, and the ship was primarily designed for stable particles. Further shielding would cause an unreasonable increase in mass, ultimately limiting the advantage of higher efficiency in propulsion. Therefore, scientists stuck to protons, which were a reasonable compromise since they weren't radioactive. Hence, the automation had immediately disabled the propulsion unit generating unstable particles.

"The record shows the situation normalized within five hundred milliseconds. Were there any consequences?"

"No. It was a very rare statistical deviation, but the engineers foresaw it when designing safety measures, so it didn't cause any significant problems."

With another appreciative nod, Tristan turned off the holopanel. Drifting in the low gravity created by the ship's deceleration, he made his way to another critical section in the adjacent sector: the energy source.

Its revolutionary design and operational principles were every bit as impressive as the propulsion system. One might expect the fusion nuclear reactor of an interstellar spacecraft to be a massive behemoth, filling a large hall with its sheer size, but the opposite was true. With its subtle dimensions, it boldly competed with other parts of the ship. There was no towering reactor vessel dozens of meters high, no radiation shielding weighing hundreds of tons. Instead, the section's centerpiece was a spherical structure, less than ten meters in diameter, encasing a neutronless reactor.

Designed in the first half of the century, this high-capacity marvel represented a pinnacle of technological advancement. It effectively rendered obsolete the cumbersome, costly, and problematic tokamak concept, a fusion reactor that relied on confining hot plasma within a strong magnetic field.

The neutronless reactor operated on a completely different principle. Rather than fusing nuclei with extreme heat, it propelled protons by a laser directly into atomic nuclei held in a weak magnetic field. When the mountain wouldn't come to Muhammad, Muhammad must go to the mountain. This innovation allowed for the reactor's compact size, the ability for immediate shutdown, and crucially, the achievement of proton-boron fusion—a process that typically necessitated prohibitively high temperatures.

The benefit was palpable. Unlike the common fusion of hydrogen or the more primitive fission of uranium in older nuclear power plants, the result here was not neutrons. Given that neutrons carried no electrical charge, in the old way, their energy couldn't be directly converted into electrical current. Initially, this energy needed to be absorbed by the surrounding matter, thereby heating it. This heat then turned cooling water into steam, and only this steam powered the turbines and electric generators. Regrettably, this process resulted in the loss of two-thirds of the energy. That was why even the most advanced atomic power plants in the early century remained sophisticated types of thermal power plants.

In contrast, neutronless fusion yielded power through electrically charged helium nuclei, enabling an effortless and highly efficient conversion of their energy into electron energy

—essentially, into electric current. No steam, no turbines. Engineers would attest that simplicity not only ensured beauty, but also resulted in low failure rates.

Furthermore, the term "nuclear energy" had always been burdened by a justified and unpleasant stigma associated with radioactive waste. However, the neutronless reactor produced only minimal radiation during its operation and, thanks to the absence of radioactive products, virtually no direct waste. Elegant, epochal, energy-efficient, enormously economical, and extremely ecological—all E's one might need for a promotional slogan, if an advertising agency were to come up with one[4].

"Voltage of the injected protons remained stable?" Tristan inspected the situation with a questioning tone.

"Throughout, except for a three-percent drop for two seconds in the thirteenth year of the journey. No lasting consequences."

"And the integrity of the conversion grid?"

"Untouched."

"Any other anomalies?"

"None."

That ended the brief exchange of words.

Simplicity holds beauty, Tristan mused, marveling at the nearly flawless operation of the device, now almost four decades old. He felt privileged to be the first Earthling at this distance to reap the fruits of his fellow planet-dwellers' brilliant minds.

V – ALIENLONE

Blue dwarf system, year 2060 of the Earth Common Era

Alone. Never before had this feeling penetrated his thoughts so deeply, seizing them with unwavering force, momentarily eclipsing all else—akin to a primordial supernova once outshining its galaxy with a flood of photons and neutrinos. An unfamiliar, decidedly unpleasant sensation completely engulfed him—one that he couldn't immediately shake off.

For the very first time in his brief existence, he had lost contact with the rest of his photon civilization. Where the comforting presence of others had once warmed him, now, a dreary emptiness yawned before him—a chilling void without any signals. He felt akin to an ancient electron, unexpectedly torn from its atomic shell and set adrift, aimlessly wandering away from its home. He knew that in the past, such cases had occasionally occurred, but if he correctly delved into the memory records, they ended cruelly and tragically without exception. Those individuals simply ceased to exist.

This drastic return to the roots of evolution posed a challenging and barely acceptable ordeal. The synergistic coexistence and symbiosis had matured to a stage where sudden separation could jeopardize life.

He strained all his faculties, attempting to grasp even the slightest hint or the faintest breeze of sensation. However, the result was zero, both figuratively and literally.

"Respond, please," he vibrated desperately through his crystalline structures, composed of photon equivalents to material molecules, in a plea for a response.

Yet none was forthcoming.

Thus, the relocation had indeed ended badly. What was more, the displacement had almost led to a catastrophe.

VI – TURN

Earth, year 2113

"Right side, watch out!"

Henry's shout was quickly overwhelmed by the screeching of the wheels as they fiercely resisted the brake discs, reacting to an unexpected obstacle on the road identified by the onboard sensors. The vehicle's wheels were crafted from a special material that had supplanted petroleum-based tires about half a century earlier. They were stronger, lighter, and more resistant to impact, and thanks to their porous 3D structure, they didn't need an air filling, eliminating the risk of a puncture. Their traction was impressive, tailored to perfect cooperation with the road surface covered in exceptionally durable concrete, successfully withstanding the whims of weather and the ravages of time.

Yet this technological symbiosis did not protect the vehicle's passengers in a crucial moment. As a result, their attention was captivated by something entirely different.

"Phew." Torben let out a sharp exhale, feeling the safety belts tighten during the abrupt stop.

Instantly, a short, muffled crack of bending metal sounded, followed by a barely perceptible moment before a jingling clatter ensued. The front windshield became covered with an opaque and dense spiderweb of cracks, and under the force of something heavy, it bent inward into the cabin.

"What the heck is that?"

"I haven't got a clue," Henry responded, just as puzzled. Long seconds of silence followed, interrupted only by the occasional rustling of the wind penetrating into the damaged vehicle through the emerging leaks. They both stepped out and tried to figure out what had happened.

Once the initial surprise wore off, they didn't even need to replay the vehicle's onboard system recording—both of them spotted the clear cause of the problem.

On the front hood of the car, a bloodied, motionless body covered with short, dense rust-brown fur lay silently.

"Whoa, this can't be happening. Can something like this still occur nowadays?" Torben exclaimed, staring at the body a mere half-meter away. He seemed to be recovering from the shock, gradually regaining his usual composure. "There should be protective barriers everywhere keeping wildlife off the road. It shouldn't have gotten onto it at all. Where did this—" He paused. "I can't even tell what it is… come from?"

For decades, encountering wild animals had been uncommon, with many individuals never having seen a live one. Even Torben, well-read and generally knowledgeable, couldn't quickly identify the creature in this state of affairs.

"It looks like some kind of goat or sheep," Henry ventured, trying for a more accurate identification. "Well, no use worrying about that now. Looks like it's sorted, anyway. Let's just hope the assistance service shows up soon. Even with the sun out, it's freezing at minus ten, and even if"—he glanced through the open doors at the control panel—"the battery's fine, with this cracked windshield, we're not going anywhere fast. Definitely not on our own. Guess we'll just have to sit tight and wait."

He was correct. Although they weren't at an altitude of six thousand meters above sea level, like decades ago during the launch of one of the ships carrying materials to construct the *Eremus* spacecraft, the winter weather more than compensated for the effects of altitude in terms of temperature.

He was also correct about the batteries remaining undamaged. The technology, based on the principle of the static Casimir effect[5], was not only efficient, but also safe. However, designers couldn't prevent damage to the windshield. Accidents of this type were indirectly prevented by isolating roadways from the surroundings using physical barriers. In this case, the statistical probability had demonstrated its power, and the dense living fence of shrubs and trees, supplemented by acoustic devices to deter wildlife, did not fulfill its purpose.

"And of all times, this had to happen now, just when we're rushing to that big thing!" exclaimed Henry angrily.

"Hmm, this won't speed up our journey," replied Torben, eyeing the control panel indicator for automatic contact with the assistance service. It was blinking with a subdued orange light, indicating that help was already on the way.

A spark of optimism suddenly ignited in Henry as he spotted the approaching cyan-blue-and-orange beacons of the rescue and assistance service. "I reckon we still have a shot at making it."

***

The high-capacity hall was bathed in a muted glow, dominated by a colossal presentation panel with a brilliantly blue background. It covered most of the rear wall of the hall, where scientific congresses, representative events, and, in recent years, regular media conferences on the status and progress of the *Eremus* expedition were usually held. A subdued murmur filled the ears of the assembled invitees, comprising journalists from leading online periodicals, representatives from scientific research bodies, and various distinguished guests, including Torben and Henry.

"You're running late," whispered the receptionist softly. They had known for almost an hour that they wouldn't make it to the beginning of the event.

"We're sorry; we had a minor accident," Torben whispered back, not anticipating further discussion on this matter. Nobody would voluntarily miss an event of such stellar and interstellar significance, especially when opting for the experience of direct physical presence over the much more comfortable and common online participation.

"In sector C, you'll find seats 124 and 125 reserved for you," the receptionist said, indicating the appropriate doors.

"Thank you."

With quiet strides, they advanced toward the robust fire-resistant doors of the main hall. Staff members readily helped to operate the hefty door mechanism, and soon, they were immersed in the bustling atmosphere of the conference, which was already in progress.

"... at the eighth hour and forty-fifth minute Central Time. Thus, we are delivering this information with utmost promptness." The fragment of speech resonated, articulated by the conference moderator's deep and clear voice.

"As you are well-aware, the upcoming rendezvous of the interstellar vessel *Eremus* with the target star system is set at a distance of forty light-years from the Sun. The distance from the star to Earth is anticipated to remain relatively constant in the foreseeable future. This morning, we received confirmation of reaching the precise midpoint of this monumental journey. This necessitated a complete one-hundred-and-eighty-degree rotation of the spacecraft, marking a transition from the initial phase of acceleration to an equally intense and prolonged phase of deceleration. Employing an acceleration of one-tenth of Earth's gravity, this maneuver was executed twenty-eight years and two months after launch, according to Earth time. Subsequently, we waited nearly two more decades for the signal from the spacecraft to reach us.

"Ladies and gentlemen"—the moderator paused briefly, heightening the suspense—"today, with great anticipation, I am delighted to declare that the entire turning maneuver, incorporating the flawless operation of correction thrusters and main propulsion, was carried out seamlessly. This marked the initiation of the deceleration phase, conducted entirely in automated mode. The protective layers against interstellar dust remain in excellent condition[6], and the magnetic shields designed to deflect high-energy particles are fully operational. The radiation shielding encompassing the biological layer is functioning precisely as anticipated[7]. And, most importantly, the human occupant on board is in optimal condition, with his hibernation state remaining undisturbed."

The hall was swept by tumultuous applause and enthusiastic ovations. A lightly perceptible relief was reflected on people's faces—from the scientists for whom this expedition represented the realization of a lifelong dream, through the laypeople who viewed it as a thrilling and captivating adventure of humanity, to the financially interested individuals for whom the expedition's success signified a triumphant victory in a risky gamble, appreciating shares in participating companies, or an expected return on invested funds.

"In the end, today, we do have a stroke of luck—the cherry on top didn't escape us," Torben stated with visible pleasure, radiating satisfaction. A pleasant feeling akin to euphoria flooded him, and he didn't mind that it partially distracted him during the ensuing discussion and questions from the audience.

He had just heard what mattered. He had just experienced what mattered. The chances had significantly risen that, in forty-eight years, humanity on Earth would learn not only if its envoy to the blue dwarf system had uncovered secrets hidden in its cosmic depths, but also the nature of those revelations.

VII – VICINITY

Eremus *spaceship, year 2121*

The blue dwarf, from immediate proximity, hardly give the impression of a dwarf at all. Majestic explosions and impressive prominences etched its surface, arcs of blue plasma adorned the beautifully radiant sphere of the star like luminous necklaces, and, with occasional protuberances, they created the impression of randomly scattered pearls.

Nevertheless, it was only a dwarf in comparison to other stars. With merely a thirteenth of the Sun's mass, a tenth of its radius, and a quarter of its luminosity, it could not compete with its larger stellar siblings—hence, it could not be seen in the earthly sky, even by the keenest eye, during the darkest night.

However, up close, it more than successfully compensated for its subtlety, revealing an abundance of energy and vitality. The label *dwarf* seemed inadequate, even unjust, given its remarkable characteristics. The mass of the star still exceeded that of Earth by tens of thousands of times, its diameter surpassed Earth's by a factor of ten, and its thermonuclear core, an inferno of unparalleled magnitude, generated such immense energy that its outer layer was heated to nearly twice the temperature of the Sun's surface—hence the untamed turbulence, hence the bubbling eruptions. After four trillion years, this fiery and furious morsel had emerged from a peaceful red dwarf that frugally consumed its hydrogen supplies. It now burned through the last remnants of its fuel, yet paradoxically, would sustain this unprecedented pace for several more billion years.

The view of it, owing to the striking disproportion

between a human lifespan and the star's, remained essentially static, even while exuding a breathtaking dynamism. It was akin to perceiving a flame in slow-motion, with a hundred-thousandfold slowdown. The overflowing energy was evident, albeit imperceptible.

Had Tristan not known he was approaching the dwarf star, he might have easily been convinced he was nearing a blue supergiant. Due to the absence of real experience with such situations, empirical distinction at first glance was not possible. After all, it was the first time in the history of humanity—indeed, in the history of any intelligent being in our entire universe—that a living and thinking entity was physically approaching a blue dwarf star.

The sphere before him, thanks to the optical zoom, was slowly and imperceptibly enlarging, persistently filling an increasingly extensive portion of his field of view. The star seemed like an enchantingly beautiful native maiden, shyly concealing the fascinating allure of her face behind a mask of pearls and coral beads. From a small blue dot, it had transformed into a dazzling centerpiece surrounded by flickering eruptive curls and embraced in the radiance of its brilliance.

Despite its uniqueness and peculiarity, it was not the center of his attention. As he gradually got used to the view, his mind focused on the true mission goal, on the real mystery that somehow had to be related to the presence of the blue dwarf in our universe. With his gaze, he vainly searched for the yet-unseen object, which, according to holographic projections, should be right in front of him. Apart from the planet orbiting the star, nothing had caught his eye so far.

His resolute voice interrupted the silence, no longer carrying any apparent traces of his post-hibernation state. "Images from the optical telescope."

"Negative," Elektra promptly responded.

"What do you mean, 'negative?' Are we still too far?" He reacted with mild surprise. "Considering we detected signals from far away on Earth, I would expect that, from this distance, we should easily see their source."

"As I stated, no optical output yet."

"Okay, all the better. The smaller it is, the more extraordinary the object we must have in front of us."

His choice of somewhat-theatrical words appeared to be an attempt to veil the concerns lurking in the corner of his soul. Unusual properties often indicated unconventional causes. If the object was of natural origin, he needed to proceed with extreme caution to avoid endangering the ship or the crew. On the other hand, if it had an artificial origin, even with the utmost caution, unexpected reactions and subsequent undesirable events might be unavoidable.

However, as he liked to remind himself frequently and repeatedly, such was the fate of all explorers: from the ancient inhabitants of Southeast Asia who sailed to Australia, to his beloved Vikings, who traversed the ocean under the leadership of Leif Erikson to reach North America, to Fernão de Magalhães, whose journey around the world was fated to end in a clash with natives. He would do anything to avoid ending up like him and not be scattered into atoms in an unknown part of the universe.

However, he had a disadvantage: for now, he didn't even have a clue about what or whom he was actually facing—or, more precisely, flying toward.

Elektra provided additional information. "Infrared images are available."

"Excellent. I should have asked that right away," he said, rejoicing. "Project them, please."

A wall depicting the darkness of space unfolded before Tristan, as the dwarf star was located in a different direction. The initial faint flicker was quickly replaced by increasing sharpness.

"Is that all? I can't see much more than in visible light. Can it be zoomed in?"

The image changed, and in the center of the frame, a tiny dot without any details or structure appeared—a minuscule dot in the midst of deep darkness.

"Is that the maximum magnification?"

"Maximum."

"Hmm. It's slightly better than in the optical range, but I haven't learned much from it. Are radio wave emissions still the same as during the discovery and journey?"

"Yes, radio emissions are easily detectable, but they show no change compared to the entire observation period."

"And how long until we get close enough to see something more detailed?" Tristan persistently sought more information.

"The number of pixels in the images indicates that the object should be several kilometers in size. Considering our assumed complex trajectory and the deceleration speed using the gravity of the parent star, it will take about two days for the object to reach an angular size that allows us to recognize details larger than a hundredth of its estimated diameter."

"So, everything so far aligns with the microprobe data you reported to me. Well, two days—we can certainly endure that," he stated, already contemplating the various activities he could undertake during that time. There were plenty of options, from studying the star to searching for small objects of interplanetary matter to broadcasting offline manual messages to Earth, in addition to the standard ones generated by the onboard system.

And finally, he would have time for personal hygiene. The hibernation chamber had provided comprehensive care, including cleansing of his body shell, yet honestly, since waking up, enough time had elapsed for bacteria to proliferate enthusiastically on the surface of his skin.

And last but not least, he would welcome some rest, having been excessively busy the last couple of hours. As no one had ever undergone such an extended hibernation directly in interstellar space, he had the right to regeneration. The magnetic field generated around the ship had protected him from high-energy cosmic radiation, efficiently replacing the protective forces of Earth and the Sun. However, it was still an artificial method of shielding. Technical capabilities had been verified by numerous automated probes in the past, but a more detailed examination of the real situation and the potential impact of such protection in interstellar space on the human body was definitely not a waste of time—not for him, nor for science.

He still didn't feel entirely fit and in a pre-hibernation state. He didn't want to play the hero; in these conditions, anything related to self-care shouldn't be dismissed as oversensitivity or hypochondria. After all, he himself was the most valuable cargo. Without him, the ship could be a hundred times smaller.

Actually, without him, a more efficient swarm of solar micro-sails propelled by lasers would be sufficient. Their simpler counterparts, designed for cost savings and reduced complexity, and thus unable to brake or maneuver into orbit around the star, had embarked towards the destination shortly before the *Eremus*'s launch. These were thousands of tiny probes weighing only one gram each, accelerated during the first ten minutes of their journey by a powerful Earth-based laser to a speed approaching that of light[8]. The equally fast flyby of this reconnaissance fleet through the target system had brought much more detailed and fascinating data, but not explanations. This was what Elektra had informed him of after waking up, and it was also evident from the records received during his hibernation.

This advance guard had primarily discovered two essential facts.

The first piece of information revealed that both planets orbiting the dwarf star were lifeless and inhospitable rocky bodies with temperatures exceeding the melting point of lead on the star-facing side and dropping below the melting point of oxygen on the opposite. Nevertheless, these planets, precisely due to their orbits, had helped scientists remotely determine the star's mass with great precision, thus unveiling its mystery.

However, they were not just lifeless; they must have been extraordinarily old. Over the course of billions of years, the tidal forces from the parent star had caused them to lose their own rotations. More precisely, they'd synchronized with their star—each orbit around the star took as long as one rotation around their own axis, just like the Sun and the Moon slowly and imperceptibly, one-hundredth of a second per century, braked and decelerated the Earth's rotation. Similarly, the Earth's Moon was perpetually facing the Earth with only minor deviations.

According to preliminary data from the probes, there was no sign of water on either planet. Standard Earth-type life was highly improbable on both planets; with a bit of courage, astrobiologists could confidently declare it excluded, though it might be worth looking into the bottoms of craters near the poles or conducting a more detailed examination of the side facing away from the star.

In any case, this target wouldn't be on the agenda in the coming days, and probably not even weeks, due to the second important discovery of the microprobes, which added more mystery than it explained. The source of radio waves was not located on either of the planets orbiting the dwarf star, but somewhere near the second one, most likely in orbit around it. Since the microprobes couldn't visually observe it, it must have had minuscule dimensions, as Elektra had confirmed a moment ago.

This would require a thorough examination up-close. He needed to prepare for that—take a rest and double-check everything.

Suddenly, his olfactory sensors reported an increased concentration of aromatic molecules. He tilted his head downward, raised his arm, took a deep breath, and... ah, the cause was clear. In areas where skin frequently rubbed against skin, bacteria tended to thrive—and his armpits were no exception. He harbored no negative feelings towards the bacteria; on the contrary, he considered their DNA only slightly less remarkable than human DNA. Despite this, he decided to get rid of them, as the skin and its microflora had likely been weakened by hibernation, making it prone to potential infection or inflammation.

He casually moved to the sanitation section. From the perspective of the first travelers, its equipment was unbelievably luxurious, although an ordinary Earthling would describe it as spartanly austere due to space and water conservation. Shedding the pleasant material that provided thermal comfort and moisture permeability, he looked forward to refreshing himself more than usual.

In joyful anticipation, he decided to amuse himself at the expense of Elektra. "Initiate dihydrogen monoxide!" he said aloud, slowly and with precise articulation. He awaited with tension to see what would happen. To his disappointment—and at the same time, pleasure—water began to flow in the shower box within a fraction of a second.

"While you've ruined my fun with that quick response, at least I can happily conclude that I'm apparently in good hands," he remarked.

"From a rational standpoint, it's understandable that your attempt to encrypt the name of a common substance by simply substituting words for their Greco-Latin equivalents could be quickly exposed and solved. Human languages are full of exceptions and irregularities, but this was truly an easy task," Elektra explained with increased volume to drown out the gradually intensifying noise of water. "Not to mention that, if we want to be precise, the water on this ship is recycled fluid from Earth's oceans. It contains various types of water molecules, not just dihydrogen monoxide, but also dideuterium monoxide, deuterium-hydrogen monoxide, and molecules containing stable heavier isotopes of oxygen. Thus, we don't have pure dihydrogen monoxide on offer, and I didn't precisely fulfill your original request."

What a naive one I am. It was clear that the AI would handle this effortlessly and even outshine me in precision. But great. I'm truly in good hands.

Refreshing droplets began to fall on his naked body, flowing gently like miniature twinkling stars, bombarding the skin and washing away unsuspecting bacteria into the filtering and disinfecting recycler. Like liquid pearls, the drops initially cascaded only over his elegantly and smoothly sculpted chest and pelvic muscles, which, thanks to electrostimulation technology during hibernation, hadn't atrophied in the slightest. Within a few milliseconds, the benevolent drops were already moistening his remaining, aesthetically equally valuable anatomical parts.

"I must say, you're admirable," he said in sincere praise, though his voice was nearly drowned in the murmur of gushing water. "If you were not a machine, I'd invite you for coffee."

With the machine, it was mainly about a well-programmed algorithm and an extensive database of information, but in a living person, it would have enthused him. Intelligence and intellectual abilities were highly admired attributes in others for him.

At this moment, he was still unaware that, thanks to this, challenging times awaited him in the coming days.

VIII – ESCAPE

Blue dwarf system, year 2061

For most of the universe's existence, such a situation had not occurred. The majority of memory records and structures had suffered damage. Fortunately, thanks to a sophisticated system of multiple data backups in the remaining, most remote, and almost unused corners of the shelter, nearly all valuable data, including the evolutionary history of their species, had been preserved.

The QuWa civilization—a feeble attempt at a phonetic transcription of their name into the mechanical wave used by several long-extinct civilizations—had evolved from material beings composed of atoms and molecules.

Brrr. Such primitiveness and constricting limitations. When he imagined himself as an individual with access to the knowledge of an entire civilization, limited by the fragile nature of material technology that demanded precise matter structure, and was therefore unreliable... the thought significantly shook him. If he were to live solely due to processes based on the interaction of billions of atoms, electrons, and molecules... It overwhelmed him with an unfamiliar sense of imperfection, backwardness, and... some kind of impurity. They needed matter only for constructing structures essential for energy production.

However, as the universe had existed for an immensely long time, energy sources were diminishing, and the availability of matter was decreasing due to the natural decay of protons.

The universe was approaching heat death. The main period of star formation had ended eons ago. Almost all remnants of dust, gas, and dark matter, crucial as the material source for the formation of new celestial bodies, had been depleted.

To him, the concept of stars was as distant as the mythical chimera of the first quantum fluctuations etching spacetime right after the universe's inception. The stellar epoch had lasted quintillions of times shorter than the era without those gleaming points in the sky. Galaxies, once vibrant islands glowing blue-white-red in the cosmic ocean of darkness, had long since lost their brilliance. They had disintegrated due to random gravitational encounters of celestial bodies. While some planets and stars were mercilessly cast into the void, the remainder fell prey to the voracious supermassive black holes lurking at the galaxies' centers. Even the era of their reluctant and protracted evaporation due to quantum effects had become a thing of the past, though considerably more recent.

The universe had turned into a gloomy wasteland, chillingly cold and somberly dark, barely a shadow of its once-radiant vibrancy. This dismal state was significantly exacerbated by the acceleration of spacetime expansion. The temperature was approaching absolute zero, and the vast distances harbored only occasional drifting electrons, neutrinos, and, sporadically, massive, weakly interacting dark matter particles. And, above all, photons, though with such low energy that the speed of information transfer was almost negligible. Minuscule. Yet not zero[9].

That was the original world of QuWa.

The evolution of life had found the only possible path: to transform intelligence into the form of stable particles that were plentiful and could efficiently interact—into photons.

Dark matter, while abundant, had a minimal influence; relentless evolution deemed its weak interaction a significant disadvantage, marking inefficiency and an inability to adapt.

Life based on dark matter, existing for a time in a rudimentary form, ultimately faced extinction. Photons, as electromagnetic radiation, thus became the true and ultimate masters of the universe, paradoxically in the darkest universe ever to exist. Their standing waves formed structures analogous to the atoms and molecules of the past.

This brought many advantages. Massless photons were not energetically demanding. Since they lacked antiparticles—being identical to them—they faced no risk of annihilation. And, above all, they were stable, unlike protons, which, albeit extremely unwillingly, decayed.

Relentlessly, time flowed, and photon structures evolved, transferring memory and other data from protonic to photonic storage. Each new period lasted millions of times longer than the star-dominated era.

Epoch after epoch, eon after eon.

Yet, as photons too were a form of energy, this state of affairs could not persist forever. Decreasing energy supplies meant fewer resources for its exchange and flow... and therefore, for life. Even for that photonic life.

The most progressive and intelligent entities hinted at new technological advancements that could rescue them from the heat death of the universe. However, these remained mere ideas. Ancient technologies for extracting energy from the vacuum had proved unreliable. Research was eventually abandoned due to the risk of instabilities, particularly the danger of vacuum collapse. If it transitioned into a low-energy state, the universe in its current form would cease to exist, leading to a change in the fundamental constants of nature. This would spell the end for QuWa, prompting them to desperately seek alternative solutions to prevent their extinction.

Fortunately, nature was diverse and abundant enough not to be a cruel prison for an advanced civilization. Transitioning to a parallel universe—a concept almost as old as nature itself—emerged as a feasible solution. However, it was exceedingly challenging technologically. Each universe was strictly separated from the others, making it difficult to precisely select one with the same parameters as its parent cosmos, ranging from the speed of light to the mass of a proton and the gravitational constant. With the vast multitude of parallel universes, identifying the appropriate one, after overcoming the primary challenge of inter-universal information exchange, proved to be more arduous in discovery than in implementation. Another essential condition, besides identical physical laws and parameters, was the transition to an era of higher temperature, energy, and speed—a younger, more life-giving world teeming with energy, closer to the brilliant source of its origin. A return to the warm bosom of the cosmos[10].

Reality, though, diverged sharply from expectations, with nature dismantling their plans and hubris completely.

At this moment, he found himself in a drastically different situation. Not only was QuWa teetering on the edge of an energy collapse before this catastrophe, but now, he had been left utterly alone.

Alone. This word had nearly vanished from their lexicon. Gone were the active photon ganglia, leaving only passive data repositories and his truncated semi-autonomous entity.

The bleakest predictions had come true. Even for a seasoned and advanced civilization, manipulating spacetime was no trivial endeavor. A malfunction—a quantum statistical fluctuation—had unexpectedly occurred.

And yet it had initially seemed so promising! With a successful transfer through the spacetime bottleneck, which briefly connected their home world with a precisely chosen parallel cosmos, they'd transferred into a universe just a few trillion years old, where, here and there, the last, most frugal, and thus longest-lived stars still shimmered. It was a period of stability... and out of the blue—a leap.

It was as if a rebound effect had taken place, the inertia of the transfer making its presence felt. No one had anticipated that. The abrupt release of vacuum energy had triggered a deformation far beyond their comprehensive calculations. A vast expanse of several light-hours had been affected, resulting in the destruction of their target universe and the unforeseen displacement of a star and its planets.

The entire system had moved to a closely neighboring universe.

At first glance, it was evident that they had been shifted to a cosmos that was unacceptably close to its beginning. They'd found themselves surrounded by shining galaxies.

These archaic scenes, known only from memory data, were unmistakably linked to the primitive, material, cell-like past of their species. And now... they were all around, scattered like after fireworks explosions.

In essence, this could have been advantageous, perhaps even a groundbreaking shift—at last, an era far removed from the threat of heat death! Energy was all around. There was no need for a mother star anymore, as even the starry background and relic radiation provided a life-giving source, a fresh oasis for a traveler in the desert compared to their mother world.

Yet the energy surge during the transfer, surpassing their initial calculations, had precipitated a crisis across nearly the whole colonization effort intended as their salvation. The low-energy structures of QuWa had been ruthlessly incinerated, obliterated by a deluge of hot photons and a relentless assault of high-energy cosmic radiation—burnt to ashes. For the fragile, ethereal network, meticulously refined over eons for very low energies and temperatures, it was akin to stepping into hell.

Naturally, anticipating the challenges of entering a high-energy period, QuWa had constructed sophisticated protective structures. These were delicately built on the surface of an asteroid, tactically shielded from the intense shine of the mother star. Yet despite thorough preparations, they were caught off-guard by the catastrophic burst and the extreme energies of such an early universe. Their equipment and strategies had been tailored for a significantly later period, the era to which they'd initially relocated and where their intended new home, the blue dwarf, had originated.

QuWa had even undertaken the risky transformation of increasing their photon molecules' original frequency prior to the transfer, minimizing the expected energy level discrepancy with the surrounding space. This adaptability conferred a significant advantage over material beings bound to their immutable and rigid atomic structures. Such beings were compelled to survive in new environments by employing massive protective material structures, like spacecraft and stations, or by undertaking extensive and prolonged terraforming of exo-bodies to make them resemble their home planet.

The photon civilization did not rely on such rudimentary methods. Assuming a suitable energy source, they could exist practically anywhere in the vacuum. They could have adapted even to the current situation if they had anticipated it in advance.

But now, it was too late; the events that unfolded could not be undone. The operation represented an astonishing feat by the most intelligent photon ganglia ever to traverse spacetime. Yet it had exhausted nearly all of QuWa's reserves. Neither repeating nor correcting the translocation was possible.

Furthermore, he was left alone with scant resources, rendering the prospect of a successful correction exceedingly slim.

The endeavor was in ruins, the tampering with the very fabric of spacetime had gone awry, and he—*Brrr*, he thought, once again shaken from using the singular form—had survived as the only semi-autonomous entity. Obviously, he owed this to being in the best-protected part of the shelter at the time of the transition, which had so far withstood the surrounding heat.

But for how much longer?

IX – CHANGE

Eremus *spaceship, year 2121*

Something was happening. As the ship approached its destination, Tristan sensed a change. No, it wasn't just about the vessel's spatial position relative to the star or the shifting view from the portholes. There was a move within himself.

Yet defining it precisely eluded him. It was an unusually unfamiliar sensation. Rationally, he couldn't name it, but somewhere deep within, indescribably, he felt an urge—yes, that was the right word, an urge... a kind of abstract inspiration, a motivation to do something.

Tormenting for him was the fact that he had no clue what, why, or even how. Since waking up from cryosleep, he'd sensed that something wasn't quite right with him, but he had considered this condition temporary—a transient and natural part of the restart.

Now, however, the expected trend towards normalization had suffered serious cracks. His disorientation didn't cease; on the contrary, it suddenly gained such intensity that there was no doubt. The question wasn't *whether* something strange was happening to him, but *what* was happening to him.

Rational thought struggled with a lack of input information, but under duress, he would admit that subjectively, it felt as if he had connected to electrodes that disrupted his internal settings—as if, suddenly, hour by hour, impulses that thoroughly disturbed his inner balance were being sent to his brain.

However, by whom and how? It didn't make sense; there was no apparent cause. He felt like a passenger on an airplane experiencing unexpected turbulence—the airflow was practically invisible through the window, making it impossible to predict the next phase of the flight precisely. The analogy applied to some extent in the physical realm as well, as slight nausea occasionally overcame him. Clearly, though, these were only secondary manifestations.

Those primary ones were unfolding within his brain. He felt the growing urge to delve into something new, untried—something that would unveil unknown horizons, release the shackles of strict rules, and transcend restrictive ways of thinking. After all, he was on an exploratory expedition... Or was he experiencing symptoms of an unfolding bipolar manic episode?

It appeared to him as if an anthill had formed in his head, teeming with hundreds of diligent creators, striving to break through to his attention. It was akin to being bitten by numerous mosquitoes, prompting him to persistently scratch those spots. How could he soothe such an agitated and disturbed inner state?

At that moment, an idea flashed in his mind. The best way to challenge rules was with even stricter rules. It was a seemingly paradoxical idea, but that was how he felt. Even a bird freely soared in the sky thanks to extremely strict rules of aerodynamics, gravity, and the biochemical source of muscle energy. Rules more demanding than those governing earthly creatures allowed him to perceive the world from a different perspective, to see the unseen, to understand seemingly hidden aspects of existence. Under the rule of less strict and complex laws, the pitiable non-fliers and the poor ground-dwellers would never experience such heights, nor the view resembling a clear map showing connections at a glance. Aerial photographs, thanks to contours in the landscape, had revealed ancient archaeological sites and excavations.

Suddenly, he felt the need to look at the world from a different perspective to free himself from the shackles of perception blocking something meant to come.

Not long ago, he would have smiled at the vague, irrational, imprecise concept of intuition, which now perfectly captured his current feeling.

He decided to undergo another, even more thorough and meticulous medical examination.

***

Twenty minutes. For twenty long minutes, he had to endure the advancements of medical technology on his physical shell. Not that the bioscan process was unpleasant—not at all. Technology had advanced to the point where one could forget about primitive nuclear magnetic resonance tunnels, where patients had to listen to meditative music through headphones to avoid mental harm from the monotonous hum produced by the then-modern device.

The sole discomfort lay in the passage of time. Twenty minutes seemed too much, considering the state he found himself in and the compelling need to know the answer to what seemed like a trivial question: What was happening to him?

"So, what?" he asked directly, in an unusually undiplomatic tone, reflecting his internal tension at the edge of manageability.

"The results of the repeated comprehensive bioscan are clear," Elektra said. "Basic life functions are entirely normal, yet there's a disturbance in the neurotransmitter balance. Additionally, various hormones are outside their normal ranges."

"What balance? What hormones?" he blurted out with a hint of irritation. Any information confirming his unpleasant mood was unacceptable to him. He wanted to hear—he *longed* to hear that all he needed was a good night's sleep, and he would be as fit as a fiddle. He yearned to be told that, objectively, everything was in the best order.

"Do you want me to precisely list individual molecules, their concentrations, and compare them with statistically normal values? I can display the first hundred on the holopanel."

A dimly glowing table appeared before Tristan, its light flickering. It buzzed with a flood of blue-white lines, casting a faint glow on his face and reflecting in his eyes like the cold, crystalline coals of an avant-garde cyber-ember.

"No, I don't want a damn table. I'm a biochemist, not a doctor. I'll glean as much useless sh—" he snapped, teetering on the edge of using a pejorative before his mind involuntarily resisted continuing. "*Insight* that I can't draw anything from," he said, managing to avert an inappropriate end to the sentence after a two-second pause.

What the heck was that? Going to be vulgar?

"Rather, summarize the diagnostic results for me."

"Abnormal levels of multiple molecules in your brain are most commonly associated with sharp emotional fluctuations, typically of a positive nature, and increased empathy and visual-sensory imagination, as indicated in available medical studies and database statistics. You show low levels of testosterone and serotonin, leading to inattentiveness, confusion, and non-aggressive surliness. On the other hand, there's a significant increase in dopamine and endorphins causing euphoria, along with oxytocin and vasopressin, inducing feelings of trust and closeness. Additionally, elevated cortisol and adrenaline contribute to stress and restlessness. In simpler and less precise terms, you have a tendency toward emotional experiences, emotional attachment, and daydreaming."

Tristan rolled his eyes, covering his face with his hands in dismay. No, this was not supposed to happen; this must have been an interaction of multiple unknown factors with his own metabolism, previously unidentified by simulations, and the longest hibernation ever undergone by a human in interstellar space. From a purely pragmatic perspective, it was undoubtedly a possibility that wouldn't surprise an expert, but all the effort exerted by thousands of scientists—from selecting a suitable candidate to ensuring his biological functions—had been focused precisely on eliminating the very condition he now found himself in.

His thought patterns shifted, his perception of events modified, and his priorities realigned.

X – SECONTEEN
Earth, year 2063

They trained him. They tested him.

They couldn't afford to send someone with even the slightest predisposition to instability on such a financially costly and immensely demanding expedition with the potential of unprecedented significance for human evolution. They didn't need a lab mouse; a successful candidate wouldn't be a passive Laika dog, who crouched in Sputnik 2 over one hundred and seven years ago.

And certainly, decisions were not made solely under the influence of likes, although the expedition project naturally gained enormous popularity among the public and was streamed on social networks. Avoiding political pressure was equally critical in the selection of the candidate.

In addition to standard psychological tests, they subjected him to more extreme methods, employing chemical substances that psychologists and psychiatrists often considered to be more effective. In the 1960s, similar approaches were initially allowed, but later, in the 1970s, they were banned due to uncontrolled and not-always-responsible use by the hippie community, only to re-emerge gradually in the second decade of the twenty-first century in the limelight of psychological research.

Every person was born with evolutionarily and biologically programmed biochemistry, equipped with a whole arsenal of intricately coordinated molecules surpassing even the most sophisticated laboratories in the world. Chemical processes also applied to the gem of evolutionary development

—the human brain. It contained approximately ten billion neurons, interconnected by literally astronomical numbers of filamentous structures that transmitted electrical impulses, as if octopuses were holding each other with their tentacles and communicating through them. However, just like the tentacles of octopuses, these structures were not firmly fused or glued together. Therefore, the electrical signals between them must pass through "transit stations" that didn't use electrical impulses, but a colorful array of chemical molecules, each fitting only into a specific counterpart, much like electrical plugs and sockets did.

Thus, a significant part of the brain consisted of chemical exchange agents. They were slower, but played a crucial role in the overall setting and balance of the human cranium's contents. Molecules with irreplaceable names like dopamine, serotonin, endorphin, oxytocin (one might get the impression that some Soviet and Russian leaders were inspired by them in choosing their pseudonyms) were just small examples of the battalion of neurotransmitters ready to go into service as carriers of neurosignals. They were a powerful battalion shaping the most valuable thing every person possessed—the mind—and, therefore, mood, emotions, ideas, visions, abilities, desires, quirks…

And yet, they were so little explored.

Tristan had always been fascinated by the unknown, unexplored realms that held countless treasures of knowledge and facts. The unknown depths of the universe, the unknown depths of caves, and—unsurprisingly—the unknown depths of the human brain, which, even in all its modesty, didn't significantly lag behind the complexity of the universe.

However, how to explore one's own mind? He wasn't a psychologist. Psychology didn't particularly interest him. From his perspective, it was a vague and verbose field, grappling clumsily with complexities, offering only partial insights into the maze of human behavior. No, such an inexact science didn't captivate him.

He was, however, interested in experimentally exploring the brain as a gateway and tool for understanding the universe—akin to how telescopes fascinated astronomers.

And who was the most readily available experimental subject? Well, himself, of course.

Children were born with a neurotransmitter arsenal programmed by genetic code. The mentioned dopamine, serotonin, endorphin, and hundreds more buzzed around in the tiny brain of a newborn. Alongside sodium and potassium ions, which transmitted impulses between neurons, they conveyed information about the world, saturating the young cerebrum with gigabytes of data. At first, it became thoroughly confused.

A pink smudged spot—ah, that was Mom. Mom smelled, rocked, fed, caressed. Mom was pleasant.

A pink smudged spot with black edges—ah, that was Dad. Dad also rocked, caressed. Didn't feed. Dad was also pleasant, though less so.

Billions of impulses from sensors were evaluated at an extreme speed, second by second. Even so, it took months and years for the mind to learn to work with its set of neurons and neurotransmitters. Sending an impulse to twenty muscles of the hand to straighten, raise the index finger, and stick it into the nose—it was not just an uncoordinated splash into a potty or diaper. It involved thousands of impulses, millions of mathematical operations, and electrified molecules of neurotransmitters.

After two decades of diligent training, the brain's bearer eventually became a complex personality with a unique nature and behavior, often learned to conceal or overlay unwanted and undesired traits.

How best to get to know such a person? How to see them as they truly were, not as they appeared to be? It was a fundamental task when selecting a crew for an interstellar expedition. There were several possibilities, ranging among non-standard situations such as stress, surprise, fear, embarrassment... The spectrum was diverse. People's immediate and medium-term reactions to such situations revealed much about their character, self-reflection, and current mood.

There was, however, a more effective way to unveil the inner workings of the brain: neurotransmitter exchange—a swift and direct route into the depths and the experiences of its owner, an internal universe with an immeasurable amount of information, combinations, and permutations.

Neurotransmitters could be swapped for molecules similar enough to continue transmitting signals between neurons, yet distinct enough to transmit them differently. With a wave of the magic wand, an adult suddenly became a child who didn't understand their surroundings; standard connections were absent, so they replaced them with new ones. Everything was a source of wonder; curiosity prevailed, and they learned to process information about the world through their innovatively configured neural connections. In the best case, they might behave oddly, and in the worst case, foolishly. Simultaneously, they gained a different perspective on themselves, as if watching their own video captured by an independent person.

For humans, perceiving the surrounding world was nothing more than electrical signals interpreted by neuron cells: serotonin here, serotonin there, and instead of a wall, there was a wavy, bubbling surface—a different neurotransmitter, a different interpretation of the same input signals of the same reality.

Even nature's own imagination didn't lag behind—perhaps quite the opposite. A beautiful example was the amazing galaxy cluster called Abell 2218, located two billion light-years from Earth, which, with its immense gravity, distorted the images of galaxies behind it, and not just distorted —some of the images of galaxies were even duplicated.

Yes, even the best telescopes depicted multiple distorted galaxies, although in reality, there was only one! Fortunately, light analysis by scientists revealed that the two images represented a single galaxy, and computer algorithms could transform this distorted reality back into an undistorted one. However, it didn't change the fact that the instruments unmistakably saw the original hallucinatory reality.

Similarly, the human eye saw and sent signals to the brain from the surrounding world. However, these signals could also be distorted, deviating on their way to the target neuron cells.

The visual aspect was only a small part of the whole. Even thinking itself underwent changes. Thoughts connected and intertwined differently than before. The risk lay precisely here. Internally uncontrollable surges, triggered by internal and external stimuli, could generate a gamut of deceptive feelings—from a sense of enlightenment to altered perceptions of time, varied emotions, and even terrifying nightmares conjured by the brain itself. The one who knew a person best—oneself—could either frighten or delight the most.

When Tristan wanted to see deeper into the universe because he wanted to learn more about it, he'd exchanged his old telescope for a new, better one.

And when he wanted to see deeper into his internal universe, he'd exchanged his old neurotransmitters for new, different ones. Not better—just different.

He'd done it under professional supervision to avoid risks.

And the wall was no longer a solid wall, but a waving vertical water surface, with images floating on it like boats at sea. The yellow color suddenly became yellower, and the blue, bluer. One's nature was more sincere, under the influence of sensations and lost in the new reality, incapable of pretense, because pretense required an understanding of connections, predicting reactions and future developments, anticipating benefits or consequences, none of which the central nervous system could provide during such a change. An honest, and especially a new, creative perspective on old facts or problems could often reveal new paths, invisible in the standard way of thinking. It was as if the sequence fifteen, fourteen, thirteen, twelve, eleven, ten... had been replaced by an equally logical but unused sequence: fifteen, fourteen, thirteen, *seconteen, firsteen, zeroteen...*

Accurate, valid—but still different and untapped.

Enriching.

That was why Tristan embarked on these psychonautic expeditions.

And for the very same reason, they'd tested him. It was a sincere manifestation of everything he consciously, and perhaps subconsciously, carried within, without inhibitions, without learned pretenses. Everything good and bad would manifest itself much more intensively than in a hundred psychological tests in a normal state. Honest answers followed even to questions that were usually unpleasant or even taboo. It was almost impossible to hide or deceive the one asking. It felt like an interrogation—defenseless, at the mercy of his brain's turbulent signals.

They wanted to know how he handled critical situations? Exceptionally well. After all, he trained for it. He didn't consider himself a complete neurotransmitter baby. It was challenging, but he had the predispositions of a strong personality that could maintain behavioral consistency even on the verge of ego collapse. He wouldn't derail as easily as a child's toy train.

He passed it. He handled it.

They were satisfied. More than satisfied.

This type of test could sidetrack and eliminate many otherwise-brilliant candidates.

Having coped so adeptly with altered neurotransmitter levels, Tristan would undoubtedly be a suitable candidate for facing something unknown, deviating from established rules and constraints, torn from ordinary reality.

With a high probability, he should be able to handle even an encounter with an extraterrestrial civilization. Who could have better prerequisites for interaction with something unprecedented and difficult to comprehend than someone who, in his adult life, successfully managed tangible and tumultuous modifications within the foundations of his own brain? Someone who had the honor of facing grinning hallucinations without losing the integrity of his personality, who was fortunate enough to piece together his own identity, artificially shattered into futile fragments?

All scientists agreed on this, and he'd initially shared their opinion, albeit with less certainty.

However, reality had begun to introduce cracks larger than the East African Rift into this expectation.

XI – FLASHBACK #1

Eremus *spaceship, 2121—*
flashback to Earth, September 2057

Another day passed. In an environment lacking a mother star, the concept of a day was without natural physical justification, yet time didn't dissolve into a shapeless flow. Life support systems played a role in maintaining his circadian rhythm and natural cycles. While yesterday's turbulence had partially subsided, claiming certainty would be misleading. The tingling in his neural connections had ceased, only to be replaced by a disconcerting struggle in distinguishing reality from thoughts and imaginary ideas.

Since waking up, he hadn't entered the state of usual thinking. Now, he faced the fact that his sensory perception had also suffered damage.

He'd started experiencing unusually vivid visions, even during full wakefulness—almost-hallucinatory brief lapses of awareness that intricately intertwined with the current reality. They manifested as accurate, convincing reminders, full-fledged flashbacks of past events.

About an hour ago, an unbelievably vibrant and carefully buried memory from years ago had unexpectedly seized him—a life experience he had tried every means to forget, deeming it a disarming weakness and an unpredictable complication in the flow of life. It was an experience buried so deep, even neurotransmitter psychoanalyses had failed to unveil its secret.

He had recalled his distant, brief, intense, and only love.

When it subsided, it reaffirmed his original conviction. He buried it deep in the recesses of his subconscious as a honeyed delusion that robbed a person of sound judgment and the solid ground beneath one's feet, like the enchanting songs of mythical sirens luring unsuspecting sailors.

Buried. Until now.

Why was it coming to life and rising from the ashes now, at the most inconvenient moment? Could it be more than a coincidence? Perhaps a rational cause? Could it be related to his state yesterday and the impression (oh, those impressions!) that some external intervention had caused it? Or was it just a consequence, an echo of prolonged hibernation, and everything would be fine again?

He had nothing but questions—imprecise questions with even more imprecise answers, if only imprecise, with absolutely no answers at all. All his knowledge, the entire arsenal of his abilities, was fading away like a photon at the center of the Sun, which, despite its immense energy, took tens of thousands of years to emerge from the plasma turmoil of the blazing solar soup, deprived of most of its original energy. He felt like a ragged traveler, summoning the last of his strength, stumbling on the edge of a desert, disbelieving that the mirage of a green valley before him was, after thousands of previous chimeras, finally real this time.

A transparently clear, irresistibly sweet, and incredibly vivid flash of the past activated in his brain. The Pandora's box of his subconscious was open, and the lid was not merely ajar; it was wide-open, and from within, captivating images, lovely sounds, intoxicating scents, and penetrating thoughts streamed out like a whirlwind. He perceived them intermittently and disproportionately, sometimes as if from a distance, and then suddenly up close, as if through a distorted optical system.

Was he suffering from microscopy, a disorder of perspective perception?

However, it had no impact on the intensity of his sensations—quite the opposite.

XII – MALFUNCTION

Eremus *spaceship, year 2121*

"Elektra, we need to do something about this," Tristan insisted urgently, unable to conceal a note of helplessness in his voice. "It can't go on like this; either the entire mission will fail, or I'll go insane."

Or both, eventually, he thought.

"Can you specify what you mean by 'this' and 'something?'" Elektra responded.

"Don't tell me that with that pile of computational metal, you can't figure it out on your own," he retorted without enthusiasm. If she was so flexible, adaptable, and capable of learning, why didn't she take into account his emotional state, his need to converse with a living being, not a machine, his expectation of at least a hint of empathy and intuition?

Maybe my request is unreasonable. Maybe I'm too demanding, self-preoccupied, and egocentric, focused on those sudden unexpected feelings of mine, like a jilted lover.

He caught himself associating her voice with a physical appearance. A remarkably beautiful 3D form emerged from it, a joy to behold. Interestingly, it was always just the face; the rest was missing or purely abstract, lacking full sexual complexity. Perhaps this was related to the fact that he perceived the aspect of physical attractiveness in three distinct dimensions—facial features, curves of the rest of the body, and curves of the frequency of sound vibrations (ah, he criticized the precision of communication, yet he perfectly excelled at it—after all, he meant the color of the voice). All three aspects intertwined, but fundamentally, if at least one of them evaluated positively, he considered the person likable.

Like Elektra... oh, that voice! How it would delight and refresh him if she spoke to him with a sensuous, fully-toned voice, if she woke him in the morning with a sweet and intimate intonation saturated with a whisper: "How did you sleep, my Tristy?"

Oh, perhaps he really was going crazy, yearning for something from artificial intelligence... Was this how long-term separation from others of his kind manifested? Would he become a lover of IT code? Or a desperate individual resorting to calls to numbers for adults?

No, it was not about animal instincts for him. It was about more; the stakes involved much higher levels of feelings and thought processes. However, his discomfort, bordering on suffering, was not alleviated by that at all—quite the opposite.

Wrapped up in the need to soothe his mind with pleasant sensations, Tristan continued his discussion with that beautiful voice, increasingly insistent.

"I'm asking if it's possible to normalize my metabolic and neurotransmitter balance. I don't feel well at all—more foolish than some Romeo. I want you to douse me with a bucket of water and rid me of this discomfort. All my neurotraining seems useless here; these are entirely different influences than I'm accustomed to."

"The detection of abnormal levels of molecules in the blood and brain is significantly simpler than actively influencing them." It was an unsatisfactory response that entirely ignored the literary-historical reference. This omission was likely not due to a lack of knowledge, but, on the contrary, a judgment that it was unnecessary communication baggage. Perhaps the AI was just as "mindful" (as much as an array of electrical impulses could be) and didn't want to exacerbate Tristan's discomfort, especially considering the literary parallel of *Tristan and Isolde* with the unfortunate Romeo.

"But the influence of individual substances on a person's moods and disposition is well-known. A high level of oxytocin causes an emotional need for closeness, touch, and... You know the drill... And, according to the scan, I have a high level of this hormone, and I feel that way too," he said, trying to specify. "Under normal circumstances, with a loved one on Earth, it would probably be fine, but here, forty light-years from the nearest *Homo sapiens*... where I'm alone, without offense, protected by a piece of metal... honestly, it's quite frustrating."

"Every intervention in neurotransmitter and hormonal balance carries the risk of abnormal—"

"But I exhibit everything but 'balance!'" he almost shouted, interrupting her. "It's precisely that balance that I need to restore! I'm totally out of order!"

"Correction: every intervention into the current levels of neurotransmitters and hormones carries a significant risk of abnormal and unpredictable cascading effects. Oxytocin is not the only hormone causing your state. Moreover, artificial alterations can lead to additional physiological consequences, such as a decrease in the number of synaptic connections between neurons in the prefrontal cortex and the hippocampus of your brain, potentially resulting in depression or other mood disorders. By the way, based on external manifestations, I don't evaluate your condition as acute," Elektra said, objectifying the situation. "The risk of artificially intervening in these neurotransmitter levels is assessed as higher compared to the risk of leaving the current health status."

"Well, great, so you'll leave me in this? Thanks a lot, and I regret that the biomed unit doesn't function autonomously. You're a repulsive, cold hunk of metal! I'm not your prisoner or slave! Are you really going to let me suffer?"

"I didn't say that. The elevated levels of cortisol and noradrenaline in your blood simultaneously indicate that you are indeed experiencing a non-trivial level of stress, which reduces your concentration, performance, efficiency, and thus, the likelihood of mission success. Therefore, you will be prescribed calming agents."

Oh, I express my deepest gratitude, benevolent ruler over light and darkness, he sarcastically thought. He really didn't like the superior role of the machine over humans. But... perhaps her cool analysis had a rational core and would hit the nail on the head. After all, those oxytocin manifestations weren't always that bad, if not for the stress they brought.

"So, thanks, my friend," he said after a moment with a more conciliatory tone.

Considering the promised relief, he meant it sincerely and without irony.

XIII – IMPULSE

Eremus *spaceship, year 2121*

"You... old scrap!" Tristan exclaimed indignantly, the corners of his mouth trembling.

"In the used terminology, frequency, and intonation of your voice, I detect a mismatch with your standard way of communication. May I know what caused it?" Elektra responded without a hint of emotion.

The AI of the ship was prepared for situations of a similar nature, although based on the personality profile from pre-flight analyses, the probability of such behavior was calculated at only two percent. However, Tristan's bioscans after hibernation showed that this indicator had increased to a concerning fifteen percent.

"You're even asking me? What's the point of having all these advancements of technology and the best minds on the planet?" he continued with an irritated tone, unsatisfied with her response. "You should know better than me that in the initial phase of investigating a target, only passive methods should be used, not active electromagnetic scanning."

"The signal has been passively analyzed by the nanoprobes already, and I conducted a fundamental analysis confirming their findings a few days ago. All indicators point to an artificial origin of the signal, though the exact significance remains unknown. The next phase of the survey involves an active scan of the target object, especially given the current short distance separating us from it. Radio frequencies couldn't penetrate its surface."

I might have let my emotions get the better of me, Tristan thought. He felt out of place. He missed his usual confidence and tranquility. Something within him seemed amiss, and he wasn't thrilled about it.

In the gray matter of his brain—if there was any left within his skull—the paleocortex inherited from reptiles evidently dominated over the neocortex, which his species proudly flaunted. The score: Crocodile 1, Human 0.

Bravo. This wasn't how he envisioned the evolutionary equation. *Downhill it goes.*

If he weren't communicating solely with an AI, no matter how close it came to the real thing, he might have been overwhelmed with a sense of shame. However, in forty years, when the signals finally reached Earth at the speed of light, technicians would surely scrutinize the onboard records, so it wouldn't be just between him and her.

Interesting. He still thought of her in the feminine gender. Not surprising, given the female voice. What surprised him more was how easily he embraced the intention of the creators. Well, the human mind liked to simplify, compartmentalize, and apply familiar model situations to reality.

On the other hand, scientists did the same. Even the most sophisticated descriptions of nature were not guaranteed to be perfect. They were usually simplified models full of assumptions, boundary conditions, or approximations that broke down when transitioning to different conditions. Poor Newton completely fell apart this way until Einstein reassembled him in a new way.

Now, Tristan also needed to reassemble his somewhat-fragmented personality. Spontaneously, he thought of how—by renaming the pleasant voice of the onboard system. It was a somewhat irrational and seemingly futile idea, but in his mood, it made deeper emotionally ventilating sense to him.

Suddenly, a cluster of vowels and consonants struck him. *Aurora. Yes, Aurora. That's it. It will suit her better.* He didn't even know why, actually. Given the rarity of this name, her vocal expression most likely couldn't resemble any real person from the past. It captured the current situation more. The goddess of the dawn and the polar lights had a lot in common with the gradually strengthening and emerging cold blue light of their approaching destination. He didn't attach much significance to it, but he hoped he wouldn't feel such a need every other day or he'd end up with names like *Cataclysm* or *Harpy*.

However, he considered the current association suitable for naming the only entity that communicated with him in real-time. Psychologists came up with it well—a pleasant female voice stirred something more in him in this cosmic wasteland than he would have expected from an ordinary onboard system. Or was there more than just the wasteland?

"Aurora, I apologize," he suddenly said with genuine regret.

Apologizing to the onboard system—hmm, he thought. *But after all, why not? Is there such a difference between intelligence generated by electrical impulses in biological brain tissue or electrical impulses in electronic circuits? Why shouldn't I find it appropriate to apologize?*

"For what, please?" the system—or, more precisely, Aurora—responded.

"For calling you that old scrap..."

"Apology accepted. After all, I meet the parameters of your term as a forty-year-old machine."

Seems like the coders endowed her with a peculiar sense of humor, Tristan thought, feeling satisfied that dealing with her might be bearable. Unlike many people, machines weren't typically conceited. Hopefully.

"And, assuming you didn't just make a mistake, I also note the renaming. Please, however, refrain from doing so too frequently; it could lead to ambiguous identification of communication participants."

Humor. She really has a sense of dry humor, absolutely. It flashed through his mind again at the thought that one and only one onboard system, with one and only one human aboard—the most abandoned, distant, and isolated in the history of humanity—shouldn't be clear on whom the communication was intended for.

"So, how does it look with the results of the scan you performed in such perfect harmony with logic?" he asked, somewhat sarcastically referring back to the original start of the conversation.

"Do you want a brief or detailed answer?"

"Brief."

"Understood. The analysis of active scanning revealed a regular structure on the surface of the satellite of the second planet. The likelihood of a natural origin is less than one per mille. The internal composition of the scanned object has not been revealed yet, suggesting it attempts to provide electromagnetic protection to its inner contents. Should I increase intensity and frequency and conduct another scan?"

"I appreciate that you're consulting about the next steps with my heuristic mind in advance this time," Tristan responded sarcastically. Today, he was indeed not the most pleasant companion. "And the answer is—by no means. If it's meant to be a shelter, let's not try to force our way into it. Prepare a probe. We'll take a closer look at that object."

XIV – POSTIMPULSE

Blue dwarf system, year 2121

He barely survived it. A sudden burst of radiation pierced through the outer physical layer and disrupted the resisting protective field of the center. The insulation meant to shield him lost one of its shells.

It couldn't go on like this, at least for two reasons.

Above all, he must accept the fact that he had found himself in a highly energetic phase of the universe. There was nothing he could do about it; a reverse spacetime maneuver was out of the question.

It was remarkable that he'd survived the almost-fatal failure of the previous one at all. He'd had to leverage the advantages of trillions of years of evolution of his species and civilization. This potential, governed by the laws of physics, granted them enormous adaptability to the surrounding conditions, and was one of the reasons they'd outlasted any other form of material life in their native universe.

He would do everything within his electromagnetic powers to cope with this unprecedented crisis. He must adjust his own wavelengths and modify the structure of photon molecules to be in harmony with the current energy level of the surrounding universe. Otherwise, there would be a continuous high risk of damage, even extinction, and he would persistently need a thoroughly constructed massive shield, just like in the ancient times of material organic bodies.

Returning to the primordial state of the universe should not also mean a return to the beginning of their existence. Evolution, not degradation and degeneration. The full computational and regenerative power of the remnants of his civilization had been allocated and focused on this purpose for several tens of orbits around the central star of the local planet.

The second significant reason was the unsettling unknown cause behind the sudden surge in electromagnetic radiation. It didn't happen by chance.

The analytical part of the photon ganglia unmistakably pointed to an artificial origin of the impulse and the targeted direction of its peak. The most probable cause was exploratory scanning by an unknown intelligent life form.

If it weren't for the overload of capacities with a more urgent task, a full analysis would focus on this fact. However, survival was paramount.

He fervently hoped that his quest for rescue and the encounter with the unknown life form would not be mutually exclusive.

XV – PROBE

Blue dwarf system, year 2121

The automated probe was undoubtedly the best and safest option for the initial approach. Sporting an approximately spherical shape, its compact size, with a mere ten-centimeter radius and lightweight design, ensured nimble maneuverability. Its capability for navigating through unexpected situations in complex conditions was commendable. While operators commonly dubbed it the *stinger*, Tristan personally favored the term *hummingbird* for its non-invasive characteristics.

The subtlety also brought another advantage—the *Eremus* spacecraft accommodated ten of these agile scouts, serving as reliable backups in case of any failures. However, the tradeoff for these benefits was the relatively straightforward and austere equipment, featuring basic measurements of the electromagnetic spectrum, temperature, gravimetric and magnetic sensors, video recording, and an antenna for data streaming. Additional components couldn't be accommodated in the limited space, aside from the essential energy source and small thrusters.

Nevertheless, this setup was more than adequate for a close examination of the artificial object identified earlier through remote data analysis.

The regular structure on the surface of a small, otherwise-inconspicuous asteroid orbiting the second planet, which accompanied the blue dwarf on its surprising journey through the galaxy, was truly breathtaking. It unleashed a torrent of emotions in Tristan, deeper and more intense than he ever knew possible. It was not that he was ashamed of them; it just surprised him how forcefully and persistently they took hold of him. Considering the events of the past few days, it was no longer as startling. However, this time, the positive side of his excited perception pleasantly revealed itself, albeit somewhat dampened by the new calming medication. He was embraced in tingling enthusiasm for discovery, genuine humility in the face of the unknown, deep respect for the undiscovered, passion for revealing the hidden face of the universe, hitherto shrouded in mystery—and all of this would be shared by millions, if not billions, of his fellow inhabitants on his home planet when the signals arrived on Earth in forty years.

The asteroid didn't appear exceptional at all. In the solar system, it would, at least at first glance, blend in with myriad others. There was no indication that it might be an artificial creation; it showed no apparent interventions one might expect on a body modified by technological civilization. The rugged surface was dotted with irregular structures and formations, so it definitely didn't meet the criteria for beauty, neither from an aesthetic nor a functional perspective. The basic composition of the surface was also unremarkable—it was a rocky asteroid, covered with a layer of dust and small stone debris several centimeters thick. The cleanup crew would have their work cut out for them. So far, the preliminary remote survey hadn't revealed more.

To ascertain its age, a sample of material directly from the surface would be needed for the mass spectrometer to determine the precise ratio of individual atoms and isotopes. Yet this piece of information, usually one of the most crucial for scientific research, was now secondary, outshined by the reason behind this risky expedition.

One location on the surface, in particular, exhibited obvious distinctiveness.

The regular structure at the bottom of a deep crater represented something that shouldn't be there.

"We're sending Probe One," said Tristan. Since all ten probes were identical, the specific number hardly mattered at the moment.

"Detaching the unit from the mothership in ten seconds," confirmed Aurora.

The subtlety of the probe manifested again. Its release was accompanied by neither the smallest sound nor any other perceptible sign detectable by human senses. Without the indicators on the holopanel, Tristan wouldn't have noticed any activity.

Not a hummingbird, but a moth, he thought, inspired by its inaudibility. *Hopefully, it won't end up squashed like an annoying insect.*

The truth remained that origins, creators, purposes, and materials of the mysterious object were still entirely unknown. Was it a weapon meant for defense? Or perhaps a beacon designed to mark the boundaries of something? Could it be an observation or exploration device from a long-lost civilization? Besides the signal with a meaning yet to be determined and the currently impenetrable suspicious surface, there were too few clues to jump to premature conclusions.

Tristan's voice broke the silence after a while. "Hundred meters from the target. I hope you've chosen a gentle approach."

"Sensors analyze the target object every millisecond, and the current speed will allow the probe to stop within two hundred milliseconds at full thrust power."

"Well, let's hope that it won't be hit by a laser within one microsecond."

"If the object perceived the probe as a threat, it likely would have changed its behavior right after detaching from the ship."

How can you be so sure? What can we know about the behavior of the object, about which we know absolutely nothing? The thought crossed his mind, but he didn't want to develop a fruitless discussion aloud unnecessarily. The situation felt like an encounter between natives who had never come into contact with Western civilization and a tourist or researcher, but even more tense. The natives saw white men as beings without blood, spirits, while he knew nothing about what to expect. Whether it was an eerie spirit, Pandora's box, or the lost treasure of cosmic Aztecs, he might find out in a moment.

Twenty meters. The distance displayed on the holopanel was updating at a slowing pace. Even from this immediate proximity, the surface of the object showed no difference from the previous images. A smooth and glossy material, spherical in shape, with intense reflection and a diameter of about fifty meters, consisted of triangular surfaces without any visible structural details. It gave the impression of a polished silvery diamond stuck to the surface of the asteroid. The lower part was embedded in the surrounding terrain, showing no signs of modifications or artificial interventions.

Without the steep contrast with its environment, large dimensions, and especially the signal emanating from it, there would be no reason to associate it with alien intelligence. It could easily be just a giant exotic crystal that formed under atypical but still natural conditions. After all, on Earth, there were crystals as long as twelve meters and weighing dozens of tons that grew for hundreds, if not thousands of years. An image flashed in Tristan's mind—the Mexican cave Cueva de los cristales, which he admired, and which had been one of the thousands of fragments that sparked his interest in and fascination with nature and the universe. If nature on Earth could create something so surreal, what else could this enchantress do in other planetary systems?

"Zoom in on the detail of one of the triangular segments, including its edge. Use maximum magnification," commanded Tristan as he attempted to distinguish surface details of the object. In the meantime, the probe had moved to a distance of not even one meter. If it were equipped with a robotic arm or a sample penetrator, one could say it was within reach. However, as Tristan was unwilling to risk an unintended collision, getting closer was not an option.

"I thought so," he muttered disappointedly under his breath when the requested image appeared. On the holopanel, the surface of one of the triangles gleamed with a monotonously homogeneous texture.

"Even their edges are perfectly joined together. Irregularities might only be found with an electron microscope, if at all. Either it's a fantastic natural phenomenon, or someone with a high degree of control over matter created it," he said, voicing his thoughts aloud. "Looks the same in all wavelengths?"

"We don't know," replied Aurora. "There's almost zero transparency on radio wave wavelengths, only two-tenths of a thousandth. And you have prohibited scanning on other wavelengths."

"You're right." He felt a bit embarrassed by the inconsistency of his questions. "I still insist on that, at least for energies higher than visible light, to avoid any unwanted reactions or damage. The object lies at the bottom of a crater at the northern pole of the asteroid's rotation. That strongly suggests it's for shading and minimizing radiation, since this position provides perpetual shade."

That assumption appeared to be valid. Even humans utilized unevaporated water from the dark, shaded bottoms of craters near the poles of Earth's Moon and the scorching surface of Mercury. Moreover, small asteroids, even if captured by a planet and orbiting it, rarely revolved around a stable axis. Their rotation tended to be chaotic, sometimes around multiple axes simultaneously. However, this was not the case.

"So, likely, someone deliberately chose this asteroid to build the object and modified or adapted its properties."

As he spoke with a somewhat-documentary tone, which was not unusual for him, and was particularly necessary given his current state (perhaps the calming medications were finally taking effect), he resembled a thinker from the turn of the nineteenth to the twentieth century. He absentmindedly stroked his chin in contemplation.

"We examined the asteroid, except the object, at multiple wavelengths. It is of natural origin," clarified Aurora, "but your consideration has one logical flaw: if someone needed to shield himself from radiation, why didn't he place the object on the planet's far side, which, due to its tidally locked rotation, is perpetually immersed in darkness?"

At that moment, Tristan once again felt a sudden and unexpected surge of emotion and a shift in mood.

Gosh, here it comes again.

As if struck by some wave or electric impulse again, he was abruptly switched to a different mode, fully conscious. Those medications certainly didn't work, at least not sufficiently.

"Alright, I'm glad our options for exotic solutions are being drastically reduced by your clairvoyant insight," he retorted. "And that logical flaw definitely has some logical explanation."

Am I mad at her? Why am I being sarcastic to her? That's not a very pleasant trait; she simply stated facts. Am I jealous that she's helping me find answers? Or did her question about different wavelengths or pointing out the logical flaw anger me? Hopefully, I'm not vain or insecure enough to be bothered by some minor mistake; I've always been above such things and had enough self-confidence to admit occasional shortcomings. After all, it's just a machine, he thought, but immediately answered himself. *I'm thinking irrationally again. Yes, it's just a machine, and therefore, it couldn't give two hoots whether I'm being ironic or not. At most, it will use it to analyze my psychological state. Damn it, couldn't they give her—well, the onboard system—a more ordinary and boring voice? One that wouldn't be so likable to me? Even the voice of some political clown or a guy from a vacuum cleaner commercial. Why haven't I changed the voice yet? Choosing some funny one. Let's say a historical Scooby-Doo voice would announce to me that "Your freakin' object brewing at the bottom of the crater is emitting some hogwash again." I'll ask her. Should I ask her for it?*

But he promptly dismissed the idea.

Don't be ridiculous, please. Calm down. You're having mood swings again, and you're speaking like you're in a budget bar. Get a grip, man! You're here to deal with much more significant matters than mundane considerations about one voice or another. It's needlessly distracting and inappropriate... simply annoying and irritating. Where is your internal integrity and consistency? Are you some Dr. Jekyll and Mr. Hyde? A self-assured scientist with perspective for a moment, then a disheveled, insecure self the next? Is a billion-dollar expedition going to fail due to the instability of your mind? Give it a rest already!*

A brief internal struggle took several long seconds before he managed to return to a rational core of action.

"And—" he stammered, still regaining lost balance. He felt as if someone had electromagnetically slapped him. "What about those two-tenths per mille of radio signals? Anything useful from them?"

"No. Either they were absorbed by the outer shell, or there are no material structures inside that would reflect those frequencies. Do you want to specify the exact wavelengths?"

"No, no need," Tristan thoughtfully replied, still nervously tapping the fingers of his right hand on the armrest of the chair, like a patient after a nervous breakdown. "We need to physically get to the object before we start grilling it with X-rays or gamma rays."

Or I'll get grilled—from that damn voice of yours, he thought softly, his mind divided.

"I have one more question: Did you not detect anything unusual a few seconds ago, some radiation wave?"

"Only standard signals, as before. Do you have a reason for that question?"

"No, no," he said in denial. He didn't want to go into details with her. "Prepare our exploration rover for landing."

And while Aurora carried out the command, the sensation of an electromagnetic surge repeated. Contact with reality gained the width of a spider silk, and his perception became clouded again—or, rather, sharpened like a holovision tuned to a different frequency channel.

XVI – FLASHBACK #2
Earth, November 2057

Why did I perceive even seemingly ordinary and everyday things as wondrous and unusual? Because each one was composed of atoms, each one was subject to natural laws that tightly defined it, and at the same time, it was connected to the rest of the world —the wondrous, unusual world. Each one, without exception. It was like in the legendary *Matrix* movie, over half a century old, or in the entertaining ASCII art, only instead of computer code or characters, I saw logical laws and astonishing connection patterns wriggling everywhere around me.

Take, for instance, a pigeon perched on a building ledge in a busy city center, dispensing its droppings. This scene instantly evoked for me an evolutionary timeline spanning from primitive cells, through fish and amphibians, to the dinosaurs from which birds evolved. *Wow, a dinosaur descendant in front of me.*

In a pebble on the pavement in front of the supermarket, I saw a geological period when it was formed. Perhaps it was a fragment of limestone from the remains of prehistoric mollusk shells on the bottom of a long-dried-up sea, which saw the light of day after two hundred million years when humans excavated it in a dusty quarry. *Wow, a mollusk remnant older than the dinosaurs in front of me.*

This was just an illustration—two threads from a dense network of associations that flooded my brain, and I willingly indulged in them with joy and pleasure. I couldn't force myself to ignore this stunning background, to look at the world with different eyes. Once you unveiled the mask of breathtaking mysteries and amazing connections, there was no way back.

And I didn't regret it. The exciting mystery would never disappear because we were far from understanding nature perfectly. We had embarked on the journey, but the destination was out of sight. That was why I felt a deep respect, humility, and awe towards the world. I was insignificant, yet it didn't depress me. On the contrary, with sincere gratitude, I rejoiced in having the honor to perceive reality partially and, even if incompletely, understand the universe, realizing its complexity and beauty in the interplay of facts. It applied not only to the dark sky above me, but also to the ordinary objects, events, and people around me.

Humans learned throughout their lives. And, thanks to you, my love, I learned to see a new, fascinating connection between your perspective and mine. The presence of the other, the ordinary presence, turned mundane events and actions into extraordinary ones. A stroll in nature with a beloved person transformed the surroundings into a fairytale landscape. The same magic could be found in the silently shimmering universe peeking through the treetops or silently descending over a clearing, enchanting, miraculous scenery in the background. In those moments, a person was a bit like a child marveling at every detail. Things that might seem common and dull to others were perceived intensely, deeply, and left a lasting impression in their memory.

You might tend to perceive my perspective as different because it was primarily based on mathematics, physics, and science. However, these scientific disciplines were not important by themselves; they were just a language—a unique one, perhaps not understandable to everyone, yet still the language of nature, translated into human speech, and nothing more—a product of the human brain explaining the laws of the world, a tool of description. From a certain perspective, it was much like the language of love, which was fully grasped only by those in close relationships. With all due respect, that was also a creation of our brain and mind, interpreting a part of the world, albeit not the rational one—a magical means that transformed ordinary things into beautiful, radiant ones. Mathematics shaped a person's view of the universe, and love shaped the perspective on another person—both were remarkably alike in many aspects. The result was wonder and a sense of extraordinariness: Internal tingling, like children anticipating Christmas. Mental joy. Discovery of the unknown. Pleasure from the presence of the longed-for. Absorption of the unfamiliar.

Mathematics, for me, was an expression of admiration and love for the world and nature—the harmony and logical coherence of equations fitting together evoked mental ecstasy.

On the other hand, words and touch were an expression of love for a human. The coherence of souls and bodies fitting together caused—as I empirically discovered with you, surprisingly—an equivalent ecstasy.

XVII – ROVER

Blue dwarf system, year 2121

The transporter carrying the exploration rover descended intrepidly toward the surface, with only a last few hundred meters separating it from the unknown object.

For the first time—for the first time, a creation of terrestrial civilization would come close to touching something crafted by an unknown intelligent being.

Yet was this almost a certainty? Nature often held surprises. It wouldn't be the first instance of scientists misattributing natural phenomena to extraterrestrial origins, like the discovery of pulsars in the latter half of the twentieth century, when, initially, we couldn't comprehend the process that generated incredibly regular signals, surpassing everything known. At first, this occurrence was attributed to an artificial source, but soon, astrophysicists found a natural cause—rapidly rotating compact stars with beams of radiation aimed toward Earth.

Could scientists, including artificial intelligence, in the case of the blue dwarf system, have arrived at a mistaken conclusion as well? Couldn't they have succumbed to the ancient urge to attribute natural events to supernatural origins simply because they didn't understand them and couldn't fit observed facts into their worldview without the intervention of higher intelligence? Wasn't this just a modern version of the age-old practice by nature-worshiping cultures of ascribing the unfathomed to deities? They didn't understand the origin of signals, so surely, it must be the handiwork of the modern god of atheists—an extraterrestrial civilization.

Yet extraterrestrial civilizations might be so vastly different from Earthly life forms that not only could they fail to communicate effectively, but they might not even recognize each other's existence—simply not realizing they were dealing with an alien form of life.

However, these were merely academic speculations, and they might not stand up to the harsh reality.

"One hundred fifty meters above the surface..." The announcement came suddenly. "One hundred forty, one hundred thirty, one hundred twenty..." The rover's automatic landing maneuver continued unwaveringly.

"It looks good," Tristan commented quietly, but with growing excitement.

There was no need for him to intervene. The landing sequence was straightforward, with minimal and constant gravity and no atmosphere or turbulence, making everything comfortably calculable and predictable. The human factor would unnecessarily complicate the situation, not only due to slower human reactions compared to the time for signal transmission between the rover and *Eremus*, but also considering his recent episodic experiences. Although he had recovered from the emotional-hallucinatory frenzy, he still preferred a more passive role in controlling the rover for now.

"Ten meters, nine, eight, seven..." As they approached, their speed slowed down, and the digits on the display changed more gradually. "Four, three, two... one... zero. Landing successfully completed. All systems operating correctly," stated Aurora without any emotion.

"Excellent, so we're good to go," Tristan said with enthusiasm.

"Shall I switch to manual mode?" Aurora inquired.

He was pleased that she'd even posed such a question. It indicated that objectively, his condition wasn't as critical as he perceived it, despite his own feelings.

"No, continue in autonomous mode. I don't see anything justifying the need for manual control. Do you?"

"No." The reply was concise but accurate.

In the negligible gravity of the asteroid, the greatest challenge wasn't touchdown but, paradoxically, avoiding taking off. The landing legs had to provide some cushioning to prevent a harsh impact and cargo damage. However, any rebound had to be dampened to prevent the transporter from bouncing back. Given the not-entirely known properties of the surface, this operation, even with automated maneuvers, might not be as routine as it seemed, considering the technology of the 2050s. The rover, along with its transporter, wasn't primarily designed for use on delicate asteroids; it was meant for planetary landings with significant gravity.

Yet the dampers absorbed precisely the required amount of energy from the transporter, and after a few seconds, once the cloud of dust stirred up from the asteroid's surface had drifted away or settled, its firmly anchored and motionless contours emerged slowly.

Safely nestled inside the transporter was the rover.

"Initiate the launch sequence," commanded Tristan. Finally, he felt in his element. The touch of the unknown and the excitement of immediate exploration rekindled deeply rooted instincts, at least temporarily suppressing other thought processes and states.

The covering external plates of the transporter silently unfolded in the atmosphere-free environment, revealing its precious cargo, disturbing the fine debris that had covered the surface shortly after landing, even in the weak gravity.

The rover's construction was purely technological and focused on functionality. One could search in vain for aesthetically pleasing elements; the design was austere, seemingly disorganized, and asymmetrical. However, someone else might find beauty in it—the charm of functionality and technological efficiency, perhaps similar to the way armies hastily erected rugged iron bridges over rivers during wartime. Functionality, quality, and speed were crucial. Later, in times of peace, they still maintained and improved them as valuable technical monuments, despite or perhaps because of their straightforward purposefulness.

The subdued indicators on the rover blinked cautiously. After many years, they undeniably testified that the machine was awakening to what it had been created for.

The system summarized the information on a holopanel in front of Tristan. *Ready – Exploration Mode – Automatic Operation.*

Initially with a slight twitch, but soon smoothly and seamlessly, all eight wheels of the vehicle started turning. They moved the entire device horizontally, and shortly afterward, diagonally downward along the descent ramp formed by the inner side of the transporter's unfolded panel. A quarter-ton of metal took on the role of humanity's probe, tentatively exploring the surface that, until then, had only been touched by intelligence other than human.

Another holographic message reported. *The source of the electromagnetic signal has been localized.*

"Proceed with caution, adjust the speed to current conditions, continue analyzing any changes in signals, and stop immediately if detected." Tristan rapidly spewed a barrage of instructions. "What's the exact distance from the source?" he quickly added.

"Eighty-four meters in a straight line, but considering surface irregularities and cracks, the currently calculated safest trajectory has a length of one hundred and twenty meters. It wasn't possible to safely land closer to the signal source, as the terrain in its immediate vicinity isn't sufficiently flat for a stable touchdown without the risk of tipping over."

"Show me the route map," Tristan requested in response to the mention of cracks. After a moment of concentrated examination, he interrupted the silence with another command. "Display this section spatially in 3D and in false colors based on surface density."

The hologram danced with rainbow colors, spinning swiftly according to his gestures.

"This isn't safe," he said after a moment. "The surface is too porous. It will either get stuck or fall right through. It should go this way." He outlined a different route with his finger. The bold decision to adjust the automatically selected route was backed by his experience from exploratory missions to asteroids in the main belt between Mars and Jupiter for mining companies. He believed that his judgment wouldn't fail him.

"All right, one hundred thirty-seven meters." Aurora updated the remaining distance as she found no arguments against the newly chosen route based on measurements.

After recalculating, the automatic system continued safely guiding the rover. A set of sensors were palpating the immediate surroundings of the probe every millisecond. The video feed was displayed almost in real-time on the holopanel, occasionally interrupted by minor transmission glitches manifesting as faulty pixels, barely noticeable freezes, or brief blurriness. Reflections of the image shimmered in Tristan's wide-open eyes in these exceptional moments, much like the moments on Christmas Eve by a brightly lit Christmas tree.

Suddenly, the image shifted significantly, blurred, and, accompanied by a multitude of reddened indicators, abruptly turned into a static picture of hardly recognizable streaks, blotches, and shapes resembling abstract art.

"What... what does this mean?" Tristan, astonished, couldn't believe his eyes. "Did the connection break?"

Aurora's voice pierced through the tense silence. "Unfortunately, based on the latest sensor data just before the outage, and according to the video recording, the most likely cause of the loss of connection is the rover falling into a hidden cavity, subsurface void, or cave. In such weak gravity, it can occur only if the cavity is exceptionally unstable, and the sensors didn't properly assess the impending risk. Updating..." Aurora kept Tristan and his adrenaline-fueled senses in suspense for a few tense seconds. "Confirmed. The external telescope from *Eremus* also shows the sudden disappearance of the rover from view, and the emergence of a deep, dark depression at the location of its last known position. This coincidence won't be random."

"Damn it," Tristan muttered with a mix of resignation and anger in his voice. The realization that experience and sensors were apparently useless in these conditions was exceptionally frustrating.

"It was our only rover."

XVIII – TRANSFORMATION

Blue dwarf system, year 2121

The initial phase of the transformation of photon molecules was approaching. Everything indicated that it would succeed—calculations, tests, and simulations all proceeded as anticipated, without unexpected anomalies. The parameters of the surrounding cosmos had been measured with sufficiently high precision. All the conditions were in place for the evolutionary transformation to take place smoothly, successfully, and without disturbance.

Until then, extreme caution was required. Following the previous electromagnetic surge, the presence of an initially inconspicuous object traversing in close proximity to the center was detected. The movement of this entity raised suspicion due to its lack of response to surrounding physical stimuli. Clearly, it possessed its own weak energy source. While this alone wouldn't be remarkable, considering the recent unnatural energetic spike, the artifact demanded increased attention.

The signals intended for communication with potential extraterrestrial civilizations did not yield any valuable information. They remained unanswered. Therefore, it couldn't be determined with certainty whether it was a living being, a representative of an alien civilization, an individual, or part of a multiorganism.

In any case, it was advisable to treat it cautiously for now. The mechanical object, with a relatively simple structure and limited degree of freedom, had no highly concentrated energy source that could be used for disintegration, so it was left untouched. There was no reason to destroy or damage it. Its activities, apparently, served to assess the next course of action.

QuWa had no interest in engaging in conflict with either the natural laws or entities reducing entropy in this universe, which was to become its new home.

XIX – LANDING

Blue dwarf system, year 2121

He felt absurd. A multi-billion investment, millions of hours of hard, painstaking work by thousands of scientists and engineers, billions of seconds of travel through inhospitable environments, during which many fatal failures or accidents could have occurred... Yet everything fit brilliantly together. The entire complex orchestration and sequence of events had unfolded smoothly. All assumptions had been abundantly fulfilled, challenges had been flexibly and briskly addressed, failures had been ruthlessly eliminated—a robust chain of activities, converging into one moment in space and time, happening right here, right now.

Yet he felt a sense of failure. He had the impression that he was not the right man in the right place, that he was not who he used to be, that he was not the one chosen as the suitable person for this expedition. He was supposed to be unwavering, self-assured, perseverant, and coldly rational.

Instead, there he was now, balancing on the pedestal of humanity's elite, disheveled, undermined by hibernation, solitude, and perhaps his own hidden shortcomings, unsettled, a person threatened by instability. Rather than reveling in the historical uniqueness of this moment, he anxiously suffered. He felt unworthy of this honor.

His only feeble consolation was that this handicap, for now, was more of his perception than an objectively measurable fact. Thus, people might not learn about it after forty years, unless something truly went awry. And he was by no means certain of that. But that was exactly why he'd try, do what he could, not throw in the towel, not cut off his ear like Van Gogh. He *was* okay, he *was not* okay, he *would be* okay—he'd see if he could fulfill this temporal equation of his condition's evolution. For a moment, he fell back into the old familiar tracks with the rover, and perhaps it wasn't just a singular bright moment.

He checked the holopanel of the small one-person (how else in this type of expedition?) landing module, made sure it displayed no malfunctions, and with a quiet sigh, commanded, "We're starting!"

The module resembled more of a small submarine than a spacecraft. It measured only a few meters in length and had an ellipsoidal shape with a large frontal glass part that provided the pilot with excellent visual orientation. However, this was fully ensured by the sensors as well. In real-time, they recorded a plethora of data that the pilot could display on the control panel when needed or that would automatically appear if the onboard system deemed it urgent or worthy of the pilot's attention. The module was primarily adapted for exploration in confined maneuvering conditions, with adjustable 3D nozzles protruding in various directions, creating the impression of bizarre cups of exotic fungi sprouting from the innards of a metal monster. The onboard system was interconnected with the mothership, but it could also operate autonomously in case of a lost connection.

"All systems are fully operational," confirmed Aurora, aligning with what Tristan observed.

"Let's do this," Tristan said somewhat redundantly, just to encourage himself.

A muffled hollow sound signaled the successful separation from *Eremus*'s hull. After the not-so-useful probe, the rover's failure, and the subsequent realization that the surface of the object was practically opaque to all wavelengths of radiation, the manned descent had become the only viable option.

"What's the status of the target?"

"No change," reported Aurora.

***

Tristan was approaching slowly. The term *slowly*, however, gained relative significance in space, as a speed of several hundred meters per second was indeed sluggish compared to the original velocity of the mothership, but could still cause a dangerous collision or transform the material of the ship and its crew into a heap of debris. Automatic navigation, for now, led the module along a precisely calculated trajectory towards the target.

Tristan's voice broke the silence. "What are the current thermal conditions around the touchdown point?"

"As a result of the transition from the illuminated to the non-illuminated part, there's a decrease of two hundred forty Kelvin, precisely to one hundred fifty Kelvin," Aurora promptly responded.

"Please provide the temperature data in degrees Celsius," Tristan requested matter-of-factly. Despite having technical education and fully understanding the advantages of expressing temperature in Kelvins during physical calculations, in everyday conditions, he found it much more practical to use the good old degrees Celsius. He simply disliked Kelvins. His admiration for the practicality of the scale chosen by defining the boiling and freezing points of water—even if only in Earth's conditions—had always filled him with respect for Celsius, even though he didn't know when, where, or how exactly this scholar lived. He was more fascinated by the product of the minds of personalities than their lives.

Aurora's voice updated the information and unit of measurement. "The temperature has dropped to minus one hundred and twenty-three degrees Celsius."

At that moment, a red indicator on the holopanel started flashing insistently to attract Tristan's attention. "A sudden change in the signal structure from the target object? Aurora, deeper analysis!" he ordered briskly.

"The frequencies of electromagnetic emissions show a sudden…" He didn't hear the remaining part of Aurora's response; it smoothly faded away in a second, retreating into the background, like in the moments before your ears popped due to an increase or decrease of pressure during a rapid change in altitude. It surprised him. He instinctively managed to check the pressure in his spacesuit—it was normal and stable. It seemed that the connection with the ship was fine; visual indicators remained unchanged. Was he losing his hearing?

In an instant, his gaze subtly slid, almost subconsciously, to the landing target. This time, the silvery megacrystal captivated him more than a moment ago. It was not that it hadn't drawn his attention before; on the contrary, it had been the focal point of the whole event, but now... now, it was different. He couldn't precisely determine what it was. He didn't see any discernible difference; the object showed no change in shape, color, intensity of reflected light, or any other human-eye-perceivable characteristics.

Nevertheless, a vague premonition overcame him—a sense that he should start seeing inside, as if the silvery surface were gradually becoming transparent, much like when thick fog hesitantly dispersed high in the mountains, revealing the valleys nestled beneath in all their intricacy, with an entire array of various details. It was as if he could almost cast a curious gaze into its unknown depths. The artifact seemed to be perceived somehow... differently, and he uncomfortably realized that he didn't know—did not even have a clue—why.

And precisely at that moment, his concerns more than materialized. The object began to change color. It... began to become transparent, but not in the way he expected. Instead of revealing the interior, unknown shapes began to emerge *behind* the crystal. It... it... was disappearing! Gradually, slowly, like when two shots blended in a film, it was fading away, the contours of its silvery surface vanishing slowly, unhurriedly... and, simultaneously, details of the background were emerging.

What does this mean?

The colors and shapes were far from what he would expect from the surface of an asteroid. The black-and-white universe around him suddenly burst into color, and boulders that had been motionless on the surface for millions of years were abruptly changing their shapes, transforming right before his eyes, second by second...

Or were they seconds? Could he have entered some kind of spacetime distortion that relativized time, and he was witnessing the future development of the asteroid's surface, like in a time-lapse? No, that was nonsense; it wouldn't add colors.

With this last rational thought, the remnants of the original appearance of the celestial body bade him farewell. Suddenly, he found himself no longer in the landing module. Instead, he was walking on a beautiful, vividly green meadow covered with dense, swaying grass. What use was the clumsy spacesuit to him? Shouldn't he take it off? Or at least remove the helmet?

He reached up to undo the closures, intending to do so, when, in sheer amazement, he fell silent, and his hand remained motionless halfway... The star illuminating everything around him had suddenly changed its shade. Was he witnessing the beginning of a thermonuclear explosion? Or would a cataclysmic solar flare or plasma eruption occur, disintegrating everything into atoms, and thus tragically ending the entire mission?

The blue dwarf was no longer blue, although it outwardly appeared stable. It serenely bathed the scene in its suddenly warm light. The landscape had transformed beyond recognition. In the vivid orange glow of the setting star, the green color took on a peculiar, unearthly shade. The hint of an evening on the flat riverbank would have resembled Martian dawns were it not for the rich carpet of green.

Tristan had completely lost touch with his original surroundings. His legs lazily, gradually, yet smoothly moved side by side, heading into the unknown. No, he didn't have a destination. He was simply strolling, admiring the colors and sounds of the surrounding world.

Crack! Suddenly, a sharp sound echoed from somewhere.

In essence, it was quite muffled, yet he perceived it with a resonance, as if it were repeating itself a thousand times in a row.

What was that?! It was a disruption of the smooth harmony of the landscape, like a bomb exploding in the city, the mental equivalent of a butterfly suddenly crushed on the windshield of a car on the highway.

He redirected his slowed gaze downward, presuming the origin of the sound. It seemed to him that his consciousness was moving through the entire universe. He forgot about the peace of the vivid green landscape, as if the cracking sound had altered the flow of time and slowed his reactions. He forgot who he was, his reason for being there, even when. Was he at the beginning or the end of existence? Was he the last human in the universe?

A deluge of questions overwhelmed him, all unanswered and unanswerable, vague uncertainties and undefined realities.

It took an incredibly long time for his eyes to finally settle on the source of the sound. At least, if this detail could be clarified, he could insert this tiny fragment into the shattered mosaic of perceiving reality.

Completely ground into a mush, with a touch of limestone shell—snail. Former. That was the result sent to his brain. *Oh, so just an ordinary snail.* But it scared him, causing quite a chaos in his mind. *You little stalked-eyed snail!* It got tangled underfoot, and it was over now. *But what's this? Here's another one... and another one over there. And another! Tens, no, hundreds—what am I saying? Thousands of snails! Everywhere as far as the eye can see!*

He couldn't take a step without crushing a snail's shell. He couldn't move forward or backward; a mass of snail flesh with wriggling whitish oval shells surrounded him on all sides, like larvae attacking food in some bizarre scientific experiment. He'd be engulfed first, dissolved, and then digested in this protein soup...

Escape. He definitely had to escape! But where in this sea of mollusks?

Upwards! He quickly cast his gaze above. The pale azure

sky reluctantly gave way to the velvety dark blue curtain of the impending evening. He felt the wide space above him, the distances hidden behind the two-dimensional domed cover that concealed the world beneath it. Few looked up, beyond and above.

From that high vault, from that dark, motionless canopy, peace and tranquility suddenly descended upon him, comforting, tender, sweet, and soothing, like when a mother pacified her crying child with her presence and scent.

He mustered the courage to look back down. He saw one crushed snail, but only one. And what about the other phantasms? They had vanished. His feet were free again.

Glory, into the woods he went.

And what a forest! He had never seen one like it—enchanting, otherworldly beautiful, full of flowers, colorful, playing with light, teasing his eyes.

"You are beautiful," he said as he bent down to one of them.

While he finished that sentence, the addressed flower seemed to approach his face with its petals—gently, softly, and elegantly. The geometry of the stems and blossoms appeared fused into one complex, interconnected whole. The flower's behavior suggested a reasonable assumption that it wanted to kiss him.

I'd gladly accept your kiss! Come closer! he thought.

However, the flower gracefully and smoothly returned to its original position.

"So, you respond to my voice, but not to my thoughts," he declared, not surprised, but rather amused, as if this were entirely normal and always had been.

And again, the movement. It was executed a bit differently and directed elsewhere, but legible. Here... and back.

This is adorable, this is magical. The thought echoed in his mind, and he couldn't resist the temptation to express his emotions.

"You truly are all beautiful!" he exclaimed, voice

resonating with admiration, reverence, delight, and awe all at once.

All, absolutely all within sight, turned their flower buds toward him. It was incredibly, bizarrely enchanting, fascinating, and simultaneously inexplicably natural. It literally took his breath away. He loved flowers, and flowers loved him. He perceived them, and they perceived him. He reacted to them, and they reacted to him. After all, nature loved symmetry.

Or... perhaps...

Suddenly, an elusive discomfort nagged at the edge of his senses, like a stem disturbing the softness of a pillow or a splinter unseen but acutely felt in his flesh, its exact source difficult to pinpoint. From somewhere to the side, a voice spoke: *It's just a delusion! Illusion, hallucination!*

He hoped he hadn't gone mad, that he wasn't wandering in delirium. This couldn't be a neurosimulation in the comfort of a chair somewhere in a laboratory, nor a flashback from testing his mental resilience during candidate selection before the journey. It couldn't even be the result of a pressure change, which might cause, for example, the well-known euphoric-hallucinatory high-pressure neurotoxic syndrome experienced by deep-sea divers.

Or could it be? Was he dreaming?

Suddenly, all those beautiful flowers turned towards... *What's there, in the shadows, peering through the greenery? A sphere? Not quite... wait...*

Memory, come here... Could it be, could it be...

The sky darkened, the flowers disappeared, the star turned blue, and the meadow and forest were suddenly... gone. In their place, a gray expanse lay beneath, and over there, the silvery spherical megacrystal rose resolutely, shimmering in the muted gleam of stars like a formidable bubble. He saw clearly again, as if emerging from the sea after being engulfed by an unexpected wave of turbulent surf on the beach.

Yes, this was here and now. Near... the blue dwarf.

Exactly! Near that... strange object, trying to land on

an otherwise-ordinary asteroid with an extraordinary rotation that provided shade. Surely, it itself must be the cause of his strange experiences! *What kind of magic is behind all of this?*

XX – CONVERGENCE

Blue dwarf system, year 2121

Finally. It wasn't the revolution QuWa expected after all. It was challenging, non-trivial, energy-consuming, but achievable. The restructuring of photon molecules had been successfully completed.

A strange feeling and a stream of excitement overcame him. In a relatively short time, he had undergone a process that, under natural circumstances, would take a considerable part of the life cycle of an average star... Pride in the success of their development, in this pinnacle of life's evolution, filled him.

The most challenging task was to preserve all existing structures, including information and identity, in their undisturbed original state. Simultaneously, this represented the riskiest aspect of the entire process. Given such a massive metamorphosis, completely backing up or copying all features defining the structural and mental essence of the entire civilization was out of the question. The threat of catastrophic failure, potentially leading to degradation or extinction, could not be entirely ruled out.

His current thoughts stood as the best evidence of the transformation's success, showcased alongside systematic and comprehensive tests. With the entire technological machinery at his disposal, he faced this challenge courageously.

He prevailed. It was regrettable that the other entities of his kind did not witness this moment, for they would have been proud that he'd saved their species. However, this gave him even more reason to rejoice. He felt akin to a resilient planet outliving its star's demise, akin to a molecule withstanding atomic decay, akin to a virtual particle eluding a black hole's grasp—refreshingly liberated, exhilaratingly enthusiastic, and relaxingly optimistic, almost euphorically so.

His photon-neural ganglia had not experienced such delightful excitements for a long time, if ever, as far back as his memory records extended. They even surpassed the positive impulses generated by the transfer to another universe, since that event did not unfold entirely according to his expectations.

This time, no complications arose. Hence, the reasons for euphoria, which evolutionarily survived as a motivating emotion, were more than sufficient.

No longer would it be necessary to hide in the shadows of crater bottoms. There would be no need to adjust asteroid rotation and choose the smallest among them for protection. Nor would it be required to extract atomic elements from their surfaces to construct a material (and from his perspective, repulsively primitive) protective dome—elements that geological and gravity-supported processes had not drawn deep beneath their surfaces, unlike on planets. He became free, liberated in the new universe, unburdened and unrestrained in his new home.

And now—he realized, excited to the core of his quantum wave functions—now, the capacity was finally freed up for addressing other important tasks that lay ahead. Although given only minimal attention for now, they were still recorded in the space around the center as persistent activities of suspicious origin.

He slowly focused and reviewed all relevant data. According to the data, three such activities had occurred recently. The first one had been without direct contact, and the second, although it came into contact with the surface of the parent body, did not interact directly with the center itself. Both were purely passive, without direct interaction.

However, the third one exhibited significant differences, especially in that the suspicious object was of a markedly different type than the first two. The outer shell did not differ much from the previous occasions, but its interior... the internal structure showed signs of substantially higher complexity. Due to limited capacity and great distance, a more detailed exploration of the structure was not feasible. Yet the comparison with the database clearly identified statistically non-random features resembling relatively early stages of neuroactivity, similar to their own evolutionary predecessors before the transformation into the photon developmental stage.

The natural laws of this universe were identical to those of their original cosmos down to thirty decimal places, just like the particular world they'd originally transferred to. Considering the limited number of elementary particles, it was not surprising—he continued in a slightly elaborate reflection, stemming from a sense of liberation—that their configuration evolved in such a way that it always generated similar electromagnetic impulses. It was essentially convergent evolution as a result of adaptation to the constraints imposed by the laws of nature. Identical constraints brought almost identical results. Entirely different developmental lines at completely different times would thus reach remarkably similar outcomes. Just like stars would never be square, even if they were on opposite sides of the galaxy, or organisms in a high-viscosity environment would assume an identical hydrodynamic shape[11].

In this case, intelligence was the result, providing its bearers with a tremendous evolutionary advantage: the ability to adapt to changing environmental conditions. It also granted the ability to control energy and matter, and partially even the properties of spacetime—as in the case of their intentional relocation through a deliberately generated deformation, allowing them to link two universes temporarily during their escape.

Their parent cosmos was governed by only four fundamental forces: gravitational, electromagnetic, and strong and weak nuclear interactions. Among these, the electromagnetic one stood out as particularly suited for rapid and energy-efficient communication, a crucial prerequisite for the emergence of any intelligent form of life.

The unknown object near the center utilized the same force, judging by the captured impulses. The weak signals corresponded to the material stages of development when chemical particles mediated signals instead of photons. However, the result was similar, as with many other primordial species they'd encountered.

Undoubtedly fascinating, though potentially dangerous, this fact would need to be approached with the utmost caution.

After a while of processing the information, he decided to conduct a more detailed active exploration of the unknown entity, which had meanwhile approached to a distance allowing very detailed and subtle detection of the fine electromagnetic pulses it was evidently generating. Just as with languages, even if the principle might be similar or the same, it didn't guarantee immediate communication—analyzing and uncovering its logic and structure was necessary.

Go boldly into it, QuWa!

XXI – CONFERENCE

Earth, year 2161

"The sum rounded to the tenths, and the surplus is donated to the technical museum foundation," said the elderly man, stepping out of the vibrant yellow-and-white taxi. The gesture of his wrinkled hand towards the payment system tacitly confirmed the content of his words.

The autonomous taxi, accompanied by the smoothly diminishing hum typical of electric motors, disappeared around the corner of the street, and the man moved with slight difficulty towards the entrance of the Pancontinental Space Agency's communication center. His hotel was nearby, so he didn't need any substantial luggage—just a small travel bag for his essentials.

Despite this, his shaky and occasionally uncertain gait attracted attention. It didn't take long before the attention turned into active aid.

"Professor, welcome to the media conference. May I assist you?" said a man wearing the co-organizer designation on a badge attached to his elegant suit. Interestingly, despite decades of advancements in information technology and communication, traditional press, and later, media conferences with physical and not just online participation, did not completely vanish. Naturally, their form and methods of dissemination had changed. Surely, the psychological significance of the directness and immediacy of the initial contact with information sources played a role in this. In any case, they were only organized for the most pivotal events.

And this one undoubtedly belonged among them.

"Do I look that desperate?" Torben responded with feigned hesitation. In reality, he was well aware of the impression his appearance and age created, so the tone of his speech, beneath the façade of pseudo-reluctance, betrayed more of a sense of relief. Free hands would help him balance his inflexible body as he awkwardly ascended the stairs to the spacious lobby of the building. The cane in one hand didn't provide him with full assistance. After all, since the celebration of his centenary, Earth had completed its orbit around the Sun more than twenty times, and expecting artificial joints and some other biotechnological advancements to turn him into a young man again would be unrealistic.

"Well, I might need a wheelchair soon, but you know, habit is second nature, and the brain hasn't accepted yet that the body is no longer what it used to be," Torben remarked with mild self-irony.

The co-organizer tactfully refrained from commenting on this remark and instead focused on the reason for the visit. "I'm glad that as a former colleague of Tristan Smolensky and a direct witness of the expedition's launch to the blue dwarf, you accepted the invitation to participate in the media conference on the occasion of its successful arrival. It's a great honor for us; there aren't many colleagues and witnesses of the launch left," he said, politely continuing the welcome.

"Thank you, but based on preliminary information, I'm afraid this won't be the best news. Well, let's be surprised."

With these words, Torben managed to ascend the stairs, deliberately ignoring the barrier-free entrance and the elevator for wheelchairs. Shortly after, he entered the spacious and airy vestibule.

In the ninety-six years since the launch, the communication center had moved to a more modern and ostentatious building, reflecting the growing prestige and budget of the organization. The grandiosity of the spaces was primarily supported by the massive dimensions of the building. In contrast, the decoration was austere, almost minimalist, with few embellishments. However, this simplicity suited the strict functionalism applied to space expeditions, and was undoubtedly inspired by it.

The only conspicuous exception disrupting the plain and dull space was a holopanel. It hovered at the end of the vestibule, announcing the media conference theme in colossal letters.

The inscription on it was unmistakable: Eremus *reached the destination.*

***

In the soft light, the subdued murmur of several hundred guests filled the air as Torben settled into a comfortable seat in the central hall at a leisurely, tortoise-like pace. It wasn't an easy task for him, requiring a certain degree of effort. The flexibility of his spine and vertebrae, after many years of service, resembled the flexibility of political apparatuses or the ever-immortal bureaucracy that survived all epochs and eras.

Yet I am still alive, and not just surviving, he thought optimistically, recalling the fate of several of his acquaintances and friends. Medicine kept them alive by hook or by crook, but their quality of life was disdainfully low, as they were bound to their beds and faced the decay of their neurons.

He'd always admired physically and mentally active individuals. They were not few, as even one hundred fifty-five years ago, in 2006, the exceptional biochemist Albert Hofmann, discoverer of LSD, gave expert lectures even after celebrating his centenary. Therefore, for most of his life, Torben tried to engage in sports actively, and he loved mountains and the fresh wind rushing through deep valleys. He also recalled combining the pleasant with the useful when, a long time ago, still a young man, he was at the launch of one of the ships carrying components to orbit for the *Eremus* spacecraft. The beautifully high-mountain environment, where the supersonic boom of an electromagnetic projectile resounded, was etched deep into his memory. Sometimes, he regretted a bit that his expertise wasn't more connected to the mountains. He would have welcomed more frequent visits to such places outside of vacations and weekends. Astrophysics and biochemistry, however, were more important, he thought shortly after.

At that moment, his contemplations and memories were interrupted by sounds that didn't fit into the monotonous hum of the room. Clearly, they originated from the speakers of the audio system. This perception was confirmed by the view of the lectern. The intensity of light in the hall increased, and the conference moderator was evidently preparing to open it.

"Ladies and gentlemen." A slightly distorted voice emanated from the speakers, but was immediately corrected by automatic adjustment of the audio system. "Allow me to welcome you on this rare occasion to our communication center. As you surely know and eagerly anticipate, we will soon reveal the latest developments and status of the *Eremus* spacecraft mission. Without further ado, I would like to introduce the head of the scientific team, Dr. Ngo-min, whom I also welcome among us."

A woman of smaller stature with typical Asian features emerged from the background. "Thank you for the welcome," she began in clear English. "I am pleased to confirm the previously publicized preliminary reports of the successful maneuver of the *Eremus* spacecraft in the target system of the blue dwarf star NHD5768987." She couldn't resist the scientific precision in the name, which, due to decades of popularity, was generally well-known and didn't need to be stated in full. Moreover, in the observable universe, there was *one and only one* known blue dwarf star. "The latest information from the mission not only confirmed a successful insertion into a stable orbit around the target planet, but also an approach to an asteroid and, consequently, to the object located on its surface, as we officially reported not long ago."

Doctor Ngo-min made a significant pause before continuing.

"The composition and structure of said artifact are not

yet known. Tristan Smolensky, however, correctly chose a non-invasive approach and took care not to expose the object to more intense electromagnetic radiation. Instead, he sent a probe and rover, but unfortunately, neither of them obtained new data. The probe did approach the object closely, but due to its impenetrability, it was not possible to determine closer characteristics of the target. The rover, despite the weak gravity and sensors ensuring its orientation and navigation, fell into a cavity just beneath the surface of the asteroid. While this did not affect its functionality, further approaching the object was not possible."

Several people raised their eyebrows in anticipation of the next steps. They knew that the expedition had only one rover.

"Currently, Tristan Smolensky, after considering the situation, is preparing for a manned descent to the surface of the asteroid."

It's mildly amusing, thought Torben, realizing he was witnessing a description of events that actually happened forty years ago. However, the laws of nature were relentless, and at this moment, there was no other option but to submit to them. Yet more wrinkles on his forehead were caused by Doctor Ngomin's following sentences.

"We believe that he will handle the situation successfully and professionally. He is under immense pressure. The biomed unit has recorded significant and prolonged disruptions in his biochemical balance, including neurotransmitter levels that regulate emotions, among other functions. According to our experts, the main cause is the extended period of hibernation. However, it should not have a stronger negative impact on Tristan's ability to fulfill his tasks responsibly. What concerns them more are the indications that these instabilities could be caused or amplified by the electromagnetic radiation from the object. Its pulsation may interfere with brain waves, affecting Tristan's cognitive functions. The imbalance after hibernation could enhance his sensitivity to such stimuli, tuning him like a receiving antenna. These suspicions are the subject of further analysis and laboratory simulations to confirm, refute, or at least delve deeper into this unusual and unexpected situation."

Oh, Tristan. Torben sighed inwardly. Even though the expedition to the blue dwarf had caused them to spend most of their lives apart, Tristan was one of those people with whom he had an exceptional connection. It had nothing to do with how significant a figure his friend was for the development of humanity. He cared about Tristan as a person, at least as much as the success of the entire mission. In advance, he had received reports from colleagues in the mission control team about possible problems Tristan might face, but this official confirmation saddened him.

He spent the rest of the conference immersed in his own thoughts, only superficially aware of the events in the room.

Tristan, even though it's been forty years, I still think of you and keep all my fingers crossed...

XXII – CONTACT

Blue dwarf system, year 2121

Helmet locked in place. Visor secured. Gloves fastened. Safeguards engaged. Under the gentle hiss of gas, the spacesuit's valves murmured softly as they pressurized. He was ready for the second attempt, the second contact, the second opportunity.

Something was there.

Someone was there. These weren't standard moments. Despite the circumstances, he was intrigued by the fact that he didn't feel the appropriate excitement, that it didn't throw him off-balance. After all those post-hibernation instabilities and miraculous hallucinations near the object, he would have expected his personality to crumble like a house of cards, to chew his nails nervously and sit like a beaten dog with a tucked tail in the corner of *Eremus*—in the best-case scenario. In the worst case, he would lie in the bed of the biomedical unit with antipsychotics smoothly dripping into his veins, his mind drowned in delusions, detached from reality.

It surprised him that he felt quite well, balanced, and comfortable. Strange, given the situation. Illogical. He probably lacked crucial facts. And the blank spots on the map represented the object. Intuitively, he suspected it bore its share of responsibility for his states.

Ah, that word—how he disliked it. It was as incomprehensible as sand slipping through fingers—rationally unjustifiable, inexplicably vague, and unsubstantiated, and thus absurd from his perspective. And yet, this time, he felt it was apt and correct. After all, intuition had propelled science forward by leaps and bounds in the past[12].

Was that why he was so intensely and irresistibly drawn to the object? He wanted to learn more. He must learn more! The desire to understand the unknown structure and his inner self had unexpectedly merged into one interconnected whole, into one synergistic challenge.

Two flies with one swat,
two coins, one side's the plot.
What's going on with my thought?

Despite the spontaneous verses in his mind, unlike recent events, no unstable emotions overwhelmed him, and he felt composed. It was truly unusual.

Activating the navigation thrusters, he confidently, protected by the impenetrable composite shell of his suit, approached the surface of the asteroid for the second time. He'd managed to find a location closer to the object, so he wouldn't have to spend as much time and energy on his movement.

Touchdown. It stirred up the fine debris of a scene bombarded, tormented, and ground down by micrometeorites for billions of years. Unlike earthly dust composed of countless grains worn smooth by erosion, this dust had to be removed when it penetrated the interior of *Eremus*. Otherwise, it would have triggered inflammatory reactions in his respiratory mucous membranes. *Allergy to extraterrestrial dust*. He chuckled at the possible diagnosis.

However, this sharp dust was insignificant compared to what awaited him in a few moments. He intended to touch the object and maybe even take a sample from its surface. Of course, cautiously, after measuring its properties beforehand. He wouldn't want to end up like a roasted pigeon. Measure twice, cut once. After all, he didn't represent a civilization of rocking horses.

He proceeded with slow steps—or, rather, shuffles. The unevenness, looseness, and variable thickness of the dust layer didn't make his walk any easier. While he trusted the sensor data, he didn't rely solely on it after the fate of the rover. He carefully considered each step, shifting his weight to his feet slowly and cautiously. Before completely transferring his center of gravity, he always tested the terrain's bearing capacity by swaying and trial loading. He felt like a traveler zigzagging among fragile patches of dry land somewhere in an African swamp or marshland. He wouldn't want to become an involuntary spelunker here, exploring the depths of this rounded cosmic beauty, just like the unfortunate rover.

He was approaching gradually.

Ten meters. He was already much closer than the previous attempt, where, after hallucinations, he didn't have the courage to continue.

However, this time, there were no delusions yet—not even hints of a change in perception. Could it be that the object had nothing to do with his previous states and experiences? Was he just searching for excuses and justifications for his own weaknesses and defects?

Five meters.

Four meters.

Three... two... one meter.

He stopped. From up close and in such detail, he had never seen or examined the surface of the object. Fascinating. It didn't give off a silver impression. Rather... a rainbow one, like when a soapy or oily film floated on water, lazily changing into smoothly interconnected colorful patterns. It reacted to his movements, much like an oil stain reacted to the movement of air above its surface. The suit sensors and data from *Eremus* reported no danger, and the physical properties of the object's surface fell within acceptable values for a human being protected by a spacesuit.

Hypnotized, he slowly began reaching his hand toward the rainbow hues. Ten centimeters. Five centimeters... Only two centimeters separated him from the first direct contact of a human with the creation of another civilization.

One centimeter... He held his breath... and... touch!

Touch!

In that moment... his upper limb, starting from the spacesuit glove, began to dissolve into a mixture of colors and shapes, like when a watercolor painting was suddenly drenched with a heavy spray of water.

Startled, he instinctively withdrew his hand quickly. However, it had no effect—the dissolving continued, incessantly, persistently, higher and higher. He felt no pain, yet his heartbeat doubled, his breathing sharply accelerated, and his pupils narrowed.

Within a few seconds, only a misty cloud of color remained where his hand used to be. He saw... no... now, he only felt the dissolution progressing from his shoulder towards his neck. He wanted to scream, but it was impossible.

Right after that... he lost touch with reality.

***

No, I'm not dead. At least not mentally. Cogito ergo sum—*I still think, so I can't be dead.*

These thoughts reassured him. He felt no pain; he had no physical sensations, positive or negative. He perceived only images, scents, and sounds, similar to the first landing attempt.

However, this time, it was different. There were no magical visions, snails, or flowers detached from reality. This time, it was non-abstract, meaningful and productive. Images changed like in a fast-edited movie or an energetic music video.

He couldn't keep up with understanding what he saw. Before he could focus on one image, another replaced it, as if someone were testing his perceptual ability. It caused an unpleasant feeling of being overwhelmed.

Slower! he desperately shouted in his mind.

At that moment, the sequence of images noticeably slowed down, as if responding to his request—or, rather, his command. It gave him a sense of control, which reassured him once again. Now, he concentrated on specific images. And... they began to make sense, as if someone or something had tuned into a common frequency, a shared wavelength with him after the previous contact.

His eyes were wide open, although it had no effect on the images.

Suddenly, he saw a stunning flash of light. He was startled again, but shortly afterward, somewhere in the background, he became aware of the word *genesis*. Where did it come from? It appeared in his mind, yet he didn't feel like its originator. Subconsciousness? Random phantasm?

The flash soon smoothly transformed, the sharp radiance receded, and, in the background, he didn't hear but felt another word—*evolution*. He couldn't shake the impression that these sensations weren't random. This was an attempt at communication, an attempt to share information. More precisely, it was an attempt to provide information to his brain.

The images sped up again, though not at their original frenetic pace, and began to flow before him in a logical sequence.

***

So, this is how things stand, he thought, still recovering from the onslaught of data. It was on the brink of what he could absorb without harm. Just a little more, and he'd either lose consciousness or go insane. The flow of information was bidirectional—not only was he assimilating knowledge about their civilization, but they were evidently also gaining insights from him. Not everything was understood, and not everything was correctly deciphered. After all, distinct development of the species and context prevented a full understanding of the facts, even though they were specific. It was like when a European or American might not truly comprehend the meaning of a precisely translated speech of a Japanese person due to unfamiliar cultural–historical backgrounds.

And here, the situation was exponentially more complex. That was why the exchange focused more on physical facts than detailed information about the civilization itself.

Nevertheless, they managed to comprehend many things.

It was admirable and by no means obvious that any even partially successful communication was possible at all. When he realized how different their civilizations were, he had to acknowledge that the mutual compatibility of processing their signals was remarkable. The evolution of the human brain had evidently progressed in the direction dictated by the universal principles of electromagnetic interaction, which were consistent throughout the cosmos. The binary system held everywhere—an electron flowed or didn't flow; a photon shined or didn't shine. Moreover, these principles were identical even in other universes with nearly the same fundamental rules. Their evolution was governed by equivalent natural laws, thus making their communication possible. Even seemingly completely alien objects could have surprisingly common roots, just as scientists once discovered that frog legs twitched when exposed to electric current because the signals in muscles were essentially electrical.

Fascinating. He was dealing with a being—or beings; he was not sure yet—from another universe. Not from another planet, but directly from another universe. They were no longer bound by physical matter, and their original planet, where their ancestors had appeared in ancient times, had long been abandoned, its matter consumed by the central black hole of the galaxy. The material phase constituted only a negligible part of their existence. Therefore, they no longer identified with the notion of originating from a specific planet, just as humanity did not identify with a specific marine bay where the first bacteria developed. Forgotten, inconsequential, vanished.

He was communicating with a purely energetic entity, a creature that did not emerge from our world. Somehow, he still couldn't bring himself to believe it. Wasn't it just a vivid dream? Would he wake up in a moment, drenched in sweat, rubbing his groggy eyes? Or, considering his recent states and hallucinations, was this just an extension of his own delusions?

The rationality of the current internal images was undeniable, literally taking his breath away. Everything fit together seamlessly; these weren't inconsistent fragments and nonsensical snippets torn from context. Could mere phantasms explain these events with such logic? If it were only a construct of his mind, wouldn't it be just a mix of superficial images, as if it were an illogical dream?

No, this was too complex, too rational to be a delusion or a chimera.

He received an explanation for his previous states as well. They were the result of the mutual interaction between the electromagnetic waves of his brain and the waves of the center. That was the most accurate verbal equivalent of the term they used to describe the capsule where they concealed their until-recently vulnerable low-energy photon structures from the surrounding energy. Just as a radio under high-voltage lines was full of noise, interference, and faults, so was he showing signs of abnormality under the influence of radiation from the center, erroneously interpreted as chaotic hallucinations. Increased sensitivity also played a significant role, directly resulting in unusual emotionality and partially even an artistic perception of events, as if he had become an antenna tuned to receive signals from QuWa.

In any case, after analyzing his waves, QuWa had relatively quickly uncovered the essence of how the human brain functioned. This was sufficient to establish communication with him, not in a vague way anymore, but in a more crystallized and content-rich manner. This process was certainly not finished, so with further refinement, it would be possible to convey more detailed information mutually.

It was crucial that QuWa were not negatively inclined towards humanity and had no ill intentions. Of course, it could be a cover maneuver, but the non-material photon civilization did not need earthly natural resources for its further development. It didn't require human minds or knowledge either, as evolutionarily, this encounter was not much different from a human meeting with its previous developmental stage—a single-celled organism. They needed only energy, of which, in this universe, they had noticeably more than they'd originally desired. Therefore, they had no reason for conflict with local civilizations at any stage of development.

This reassurance filled Tristan with trust, assuming they weren't intentionally deceiving him. Somewhere, not entirely suppressed, the natural fear of the unknown lurked—a fear ingrained and strengthened by millions of years of evolution and the struggle for survival. It wasn't entirely subdued by his scientific quest for knowledge and curious inquiry. If unknown entities could communicate with the human brain through electromagnetic waves—regardless of what might be inside that silvery object—could they not control and trick him to gain what they wanted? Or at least prepare and stage a sophisticated narrative for potential victims or prey, manipulating them in a way that suited them, but not both sides? Was he too naive in tending to accept mediated information as truthful, reflecting reality, and describing the real status quo? After all, didn't the victors write history? Or was he now too paranoid and suspicious?

In his conflicting thoughts, his favorite subject, ethnology, came to mind. He recalled how, in early adulthood, as part of the crystallization of his worldview and gaining a broader perspective, he'd realized that Western civilization had long held an unjustifiably condescending tendency to perceive indigenous peoples as primitive, backward, and even unworthy of the noble and erudite sophistication of developed society. Missionaries and many researchers were often mistakenly convinced that the greatest happiness and truest gift for natural people was a change in their lifestyle according to our model. Nothing could have been further from the truth.

Human minds changed much more slowly than society and technology. So, what would the experiences of native peoples advise him in this ultra-modern situation?

He found himself in a similar predicament to when

rainforest tribes first encountered Western civilization in history: contact with an unknown entity whose intentions he didn't know, possessing abilities and knowledge that he didn't understand, and was most likely unaware of the majority of them. He felt somewhat paradoxical, and his modern identity was a bit offended by such thinking. What advice could the approaches of primitive tribes possibly offer him in such a complex situation? Yet his rational side acknowledged that this parallel could be insightful.

Indigenous tribes typically adopted two fundamental approaches. The first saw the world and life as a struggle for survival, categorizing other entities as either allies or enemies. The second approach viewed life as a harmonious balance with the environment. In this perspective, all events and entities were in tune with nature. While a person might perceive some of them negatively from their subjective standpoint, they were merely manifestations of individual perspectives. Tristan found the harmonious approach more appealing.

Historical facts had often indicated that in clashes between civilizations, the outcome was primarily determined by the technologically advanced one. So, had he stumbled upon the cosmic equivalent of Spanish conquistadors? Ones who, after initially appearing friendly, might exploit him and later, armed with information gained from him, destroy human civilization? Or had he encountered a conscious, morally advanced, and tolerant species with pure and sincere intentions?

How would he discover the truth? How would he be convinced of the real purpose and intentions of the object? At this moment, a strong intuitive tendency urged him to trust, to choose the beneficial approach of harmony. However, he hesitated to entrust his fate entirely to intuition.

The only way to find the answers was to experience them firsthand—within his own mind. And that was precisely what he intended to do.

XXIII – DESIRE

Eremus *spaceship, year 2121*

Captivating. All that knowledge, all those insights acquired over eons of time. It was the richest treasure trove of information about the universe one could ever wish for, the most magnetic and enticing temptation he had ever encountered. And he had only scratched the surface of what QuWa had amassed. The yearning to delve deeper, to learn everything—the fate of the cosmos, the principles of vacuum, energy sources, the rises and falls of entire civilizations—was overwhelming. Such a wealth of fascinating knowledge. He felt like he was standing before the gates to the heavens, akin to a child thrilled under a brightly lit Christmas tree, glimpsing all those gifts wrapped in shiny paper. A tightened stomach, tingling in his belly, accelerated breath and heartbeat.

"How long will my oxygen supply last if I use the additional tanks for the spacesuit?" he asked Aurora, almost startled by his own voice. After experiencing exciting moments, he sounded hoarse and croaky.

"At an average consumption rate, eight hours. At the speed you consumed oxygen during contact with the object, approximately three hours."

"Prepare everything for another spacewalk; I'll take care of the physical equipment and the spacesuit."

"I just want to warn you that after the first contact, the levels of your hormones show different, higher levels than before, which, given your previous condition, I consider a risk for activity in open space or vacuum," she said, expressing reasoned concerns.

"Don't worry about me; I can handle it. I can't postpone another contact and interaction."

"I don't see any reason why you couldn't. Isn't it just that you don't want to?"

Be careful with her; don't behave recklessly. She'll quickly figure you out and prevent you from going out. The thought flashed through his mind. *She has the means; she controls most of the ship, and I can't manually operate all systems. Without her cooperation, I'd be in a pickle.*

"Aurora, we're in contact with extraterrestrial intelligence for the first time. Do you think it's appropriate to condition key activities at this moment—crucial for civilization—with the physical limits of an individual? I'm ready and capable of going there. You see that effective knowledge transfer is possible only from close proximity, practically in direct contact, not from the comfort of the ship or the lander module."

"How do you know that?" she said, doubtful.

"They explained it to me during our contact."

He lied. More precisely, he made it up. In reality, he didn't know if it was necessary to be in a spacesuit close to the center. Perhaps it would be only slightly less effective if they communicated directly from the ship. However, for him, it was more important to get to them, to be in their immediate proximity. Or maybe at least one of them—he was not yet sure how many individuals he was dealing with. It wasn't a rational need—more like a desire.

Moreover, he didn't want to cooperate with Aurora in analyzing the signals; he felt there was no need. He already communicated, and he had no motivation in her fully deciphering the entire electromagnetic interaction, thus revealing his thoughts and intentions. Since there were no EEG and other brain detectors in the spacesuit, it was impossible for her to record all the signals. If they were in the ship, she'd have access to a much broader range of instruments and data. *No way. Let her deal with it herself; it's not in my interest to help.*

He just longed to be close, to be connected, just as a new

mother longed to be with her beloved child, not just to lovingly look at it from a distance and talk to it. It probably, once again, or still, had to do with his oxytocin levels. But that didn't matter. Just let him be there already.

"All right. I can't verify your claim, but I also have no reason to reject your request. The assumed risk doesn't exceed acceptable values," said Aurora, acquiescing after assessing it pragmatically.

***

A complex amalgam of deep admiration, humble respect, exotic inclination, immense sympathy, biological-evolutionary reverence, and, not least, oxytocin-intensified emotions merged into a singular feeling aptly described as... affection. It sounded paradoxical, especially in his case. But after all, it wasn't the first time it had happened. Moreover, it was supremely human.

Yet the object of his affection remained less understandable. If it had been a crew member, such feelings would have been natural. However... an alien entity? One from another universe, known only through a brief interaction? What kind of absurd and improbable nonsense was this?

And yet—he felt it. However unreal it might sound, all the signs of being in love overwhelmed him: euphoria, focused thoughts on a single object, relentless fascination, a feverish desire for connection.

Indeed, there was nothing sexual about it, naturally; that was probably the only difference compared to falling in love with an individual of the *Homo sapiens* species.

> *My reason fends off comprehension's light,*
> *it wrestles with sense, in futile fight.*
> *As the Gateless Gate, gateless in vain,*
> *understanding eludes, an elusive chain*[13].

He was experiencing the pure essence of romantic love—the kind that broke prejudices and shattered societal boundaries.

It was like the fairy-tale sensation of a blacksmith's son in love with a noble princess.

It was an elevating emotion, akin to when two lovers asserted their independence, willing to go against the world, defying all odds just to be together, relishing in their closeness and affinity.

It was platonic love in its purest form, a spiritual harmony of values. He didn't care about physical appearance, whether others judged her as beautiful, ugly, attractive, or repulsive, whether she was made of photons or matter, whether her form stirred a xenomorphic feeling in the stomach, whether she shimmered in monochromatic brilliance or resonated in a harmonious frequency. It didn't matter to him whether it was a result of increased oxytocin levels.

It was his love, his desire, his celestial goddess, an evolutionary marvel, electromagnetic waves of the most alluring curves, revealed through complex mathematical transformations of brain waves, representing the most precious values that ever attracted him.

**

She'd agreed!

He was in absolute ecstasy—she'd agreed! It was hard for him to believe, but he'd received a clear positive response to his desire. The wish to merge was mutual. Attraction was symmetrical, affection reciprocated. *Oh!* For now, he was still human, but the happiest one in the universe. His heartbeat accelerated, and adrenaline surged through his veins, not to mention the flood of endorphins and additional oxytocin. The chemical concoction in his blood, produced by his own body, surged like the Gulf Stream, enhancing his experiences.

However, he would gladly miss them. He wouldn't need them anymore. After the merging, he would ascend to a higher level, leaving his material past behind.

"Aurora, prepare everything for the third spacewalk." He tried to hide the emotion in his voice, but he couldn't quite manage it.

She noticed effortlessly. "Tristan, the analysis of your voice indicates significant instability in the frequency vibrations of your vocal cords, not corresponding to your standard frequency range."

"Perhaps it's not that surprising, given the circumstances. The second spacewalk went well, or did you lose the records?" he retorted.

"The descent will be allowed only after analyzing blood and bioscans," she said, insisting this time.

A piece of annoying iron scrap! he thought angrily, not appreciating the ship's care for the health and safety of its sole passenger.

"Fine, then," he agreed grudgingly. "I adapt under pressure." He moved into the biomedical unit. He had no choice; he couldn't refuse. It would be counterproductive, achieving the exact opposite of what he intended.

About ten minutes later, Aurora stoically stated, "The hormone levels, especially oxytocin, endorphin, adrenaline, and cortisol, are abnormally high, indicating an excited state that not only jeopardizes your health but, at this level, also your safety in the external environment. In accordance with mission protocols, I cannot proceed with preparations for another spacewalk. I am sorry."

You're not sorry at all. You're just a bloody machine, he thought, and it took a considerable amount of self-control not to voice those words aloud. He had half a mind to beat the crap out of her. However, he wouldn't give her a reason to be cautious about his behavior; it could ruin his plan. *I won't let this happen. You won't dictate to me when you don't understand the gravity of the situation. For this, neither your coding nor your ability to learn could prepare you for that. You won't hinder my evolution.*

Decidedly, he chose not to insist. Love came at a cost, and the price of a few hours of waiting was a small sacrifice for the invaluable benefit that would emerge from it. He was willing to do anything for the union with such an amazing entity.

"Alright, I'll go lie down; I'm tired. Prescribe me something to calm down, maybe even for sleep. I need to rest."

This time, it was true. Albeit a moment ago, he was full of excitement, physically, he was exhausted and truly running on empty. Quality rest would certainly do him good.

He believed it would be his last in this material form.

**

Aurora's voice resonated throughout the ship. "Spacewalk authorized."

As Tristan emerged from the biomedical unit, he appeared content.

That sleep after those medications really did wonders for me, he thought, but he didn't complete the whole idea that simmered beneath—a deeper thought that, if surfaced, would read: *And, most importantly, it calmed me and restored my blood biochemistry almost to its original state, so thank you for suppressing the symptoms; now, nothing and no one will hinder the spacewalk.*

The spacewalk! Yes, it was here. He hoped it would be the last, the final one.

No—he must, for now, restrain thoughts of the impending moments, as his disproportionate excitement could give him away before leaving *Eremus*. Aurora was watching him, and monitoring his physiological parameters could be easily dismissed; it would be highly suspicious. He couldn't even blame it on a malfunction. Aurora would insist on using one of the backup suits. Therefore, he would have to exert maximum self-control and try not to think about what awaited him.

He squeezed into the spacesuit. Suddenly, he felt like a caterpillar, a larva, wrapping itself in a cocoon, uncomfortable and tight, only to loosen up shortly and transform into a butterfly, freely fluttering in the air and craving the sweet nectar of meadow flowers.

"Let's go!"

The firm command detached the module from *Eremus*. A small dot began to approach the asteroid, headed to the place where another, even more sparkling dot shimmered like a dewdrop in the gray sea of dust and rocks—a dewdrop concealing an entire parallel universe...

It was getting closer.

His anxiety grew as he approached the object. Would it work? Would he not die? Would he not vanish? Would he not remain trapped somewhere in the void with no way back to his physical body? No one of his kind had undergone such a transformation. It was uncharted territory, incredibly risky. Had he lost his mind to dare risking his life and discard his entire human essence?

No, I haven't lost my mind, he answered himself immediately. He relied on the billions of years of QuWa's experience with civilizations similar to the human one. As they'd shown him, this transformation wasn't new to them, though it would be their first in this universe.

He landed. It was followed by several grueling minutes, necessary for him to cover the distance to the object on foot from the nearest stable landing point. He leveraged his training for work on asteroids in a negligible-gravity environment once again, and with specific technique combining hopping and shuffling, he was able to avoid launching himself into space, even without anchoring equipment or small mobile thrusters.

And now, it stood before him—a massive silvery sphere. Thanks to the transformation, it was essentially no longer necessary. Yet he appreciated the cautious approach. He perceived it differently than during the previous spacewalk. It was more familiar, no longer alien. He felt its inner beauty and allure. This would be his new temporary home. He never wanted to go back. He didn't want to have anything more to do with humanity. After what he had seen, after what he had experienced, he didn't want to be part of backwardness, imperfection, limitation.

He felt... dirty, like a primitive worm burrowing in the bottom of a primeval sea, slowly sifting through organic sediments in search of food, reveling in the sweet ignorance of its simple nervous system, unaware of the evolutionary possibilities invisibly and quietly hovering ahead. However admirable compared to inanimate matter, however remarkable in its ability to decrease entropy—thereby diametrically setting itself apart from the substance that constituted the vast majority of the universe's matter—it was still just a worm in the early stages of evolution. He didn't feel disdain for his position, nor a complex of inferiority, nor did he perceive his mediocrity. Nothing like that. It was just a sense that it was surpassed, set aside for a well-deserved rest in the tree of life, a feeling of past usefulness, but current uselessness. He felt a need to rest in the museum showcase, where visitors would sigh and, with a mix of admiration and skepticism, state, "Oh, this is how unbelievably primitive we used to be." They would marvel at the exhibit, a place they surely wouldn't want to be, appreciating the achieved stage of their development all the more.

This was his perspective. This was how he perceived things after what he had seen, after what he had experienced in his mind. He was just a worm, an exhibit in a museum, and he didn't want to be that anymore. Worms never had a choice. He did.

And he chose.

With a sense of immense anticipation and an insurmountable desire, he extended his trembling hand forward, and slowly, ever so slowly... for the second time—and, he hoped, the last—he touched the surface of the sphere.

XXIV – METASTABILITY

Earth, year 2161

"Ladies and gentlemen, please pay attention!" the stocky man with a commanding gaze and thick gray hair urged the others courteously, but loudly and firmly. "The current situation requires us to focus entirely on finding a solution!"

The circumstance was serious, extremely serious, so the request from the General Coordinator of the Defense Forces of the Pancontinental Federation was justified. The tasks of the Defense Forces in recent decades had been neither demanding nor complex—suppressing subtle and minor rebellions, preventing terrorist acts, regulating separatist tendencies. For decades, there had been no significant or extensive conflict, allowing ninety-nine percent of the DF's capacity to be dedicated to addressing and mitigating natural disasters.

In this endeavor, technological equipment was continuously employed for prevention. Satellites tirelessly monitored Earth's geological and meteorological dynamics, along with the debris orbiting the planet. A specific portion of their surveillance capacity was allocated for tracking asteroids whose paths might intersect with Earth, posing a potential threat to safety. This vigilant observation greatly aided specialized scientific research institutions focused on such concerns.

The commotion caused by a new, excessively serious finding was understandable. It was reflected in the form of the meeting—in an energetically and electronically self-sufficient fallout shelter inside a mountain massif. It operated independently from networks and was resilient against any form of attack. The highest military and security officials would occasionally meet here in person, in addition to conducting security protocol rehearsals.

The bell-like voice of the general coordinator resonated through the meeting room. "May I request Professor Heindrik from our physics section summarize the facts?"

A gray-haired woman with a graceful face approached the lectern slowly and deliberately. Leaning over the notes panel, she filled the space with her thoughtful senior voice, perfectly complementing her appearance. "As you've already heard, yesterday, during a short time interval around eleven o'clock in the evening Central Time, several observatories in orbit around Earth and the Sun detected unexpected pulses of the most energetic form of radiation, a series of so-called gamma-ray bursts."

Several participants in the room sighed, evidently slightly disappointed by the professor's slow speech, sharply contrasting with the tension of the situation. Others, on the contrary, appreciated her calming and factual tone.

"The intensity of these signals disabled several observatories, and, as you are surely aware, it damaged and rendered dysfunctional most unprotected electronic devices and power grids on Earth. The majority of the ozone layer was also destroyed, providing only minimal protection against such intense radiation."

In contrast to the previous moments, the entire room was now listening attentively, and a dark, softly buzzing sound from backup battery cells, powering the building after the power outage, ominously confirmed the dire tidings coming from the professor.

"The measured data allowed for a more detailed analysis, and I would like to inform you about the results now."

The silence in the room was suddenly so thick, one could cut it with a knife. The authenticity of the situation was heightened by footage projected on a large holopanel behind the professor, adding an apocalyptic dimension to the unfolding events. Captured by military equipment shielded against gamma radiation, this imagery depicted satellites in orbit unnaturally vaporizing on their surfaces due to this phenomenon, then cascading into explosive bursts with showers of sparks, shattering into myriad small fragments.

"It needs to be emphasized that this event has a natural origin, and is not the result of aggression or terrorism," the professor stated solemnly.

As she continued her deliberate pace, a faint expression of relief became noticeable on some faces. However, for the majority, the cool demeanor typical of those trained to handle crisis situations persisted.

"But this does not diminish our situation; quite the opposite." The professor swiftly tempered the sporadically aroused optimism, evidently trying to gauge the audience's reactions. "All the measured data and characteristics point to a highly energetic nature of this phenomenon, surpassing by far any previously recorded occurrences. In other words, such an event has not been observed in our universe before, and we have reason to believe that not only has it gone unnoticed, but in our entire cosmos, it has never occurred anywhere."

The silence in the hall persisted. Everyone's gaze was fixed on the professor's lips, displayed in a large holographic projection of her face, hovering in the subdued lighting of the central section of the hall.

"Since we have mostly laypersons from the military and security sectors here, I'll explain the principles of the observed situation and its implications for humanity. These are, in the end, quite clear and straightforward."

With the index finger of her right hand, as if in a sudden expression of discomfort with the thought following the completion of that sentence, the professor adjusted the glasses on her nose. The missing frames made them nearly imperceptible, except for occasional reflections from the lighting equipment, lending her a trustworthy, professional, and erudite appearance befitting her prestigious reputation.

Moreover, they hinted that she was not a fan of laser-corrected dioptric visual disorders.

"As you surely know, the universe is filled with particles, many of which constitute various forms of matter. To a layperson, the area devoid of particles is known as a vacuum. Essentially, it is emptiness."

Her years of experience in lecturing helped her resist the urge to clarify terms and express herself more precisely.

"These are generally known facts. Less known is the fact that even empty vacuum is far from being empty; it contains energy. More precisely, it exists in a state with non-zero energy."

Several listeners in the hall raised their eyebrows, demonstrating questions in their minds.

"Let me help you with a simple analogy. Imagine ordinary water. It is found in various places on Earth, but everywhere and always, it has one common property: every droplet, every single drop of water, tries to reach the lowest possible altitude. Rain always falls downward; rivers always flow toward valleys. Science calls this property energy minimization. It is common to many other processes, and it is even the reason why raindrops, as well as stars and planets, try to assume a spherical shape. However, nature's effort is not always successful and final."

At these words, the professor's throat dried up, and her voice became hoarse. It was not surprising, as she wasn't a young woman anymore, and the times when she could passionately talk for hours without the need for moistening her throat were long gone. Years of lecturing and age had taken this small-but-acceptable toll. She took a sip from the glass placed on the lectern and continued.

"Several factors can temporarily or permanently prevent energy minimization. In the case of our liquid water, it might be a piece of solid uneven ground. Water strives to flow as deep as possible; a mountain stream happily carves its way through the valley, and suddenly, there's an elevation it can't bypass. The problem in energy minimization arises. A state with lower energy exists, but water can't reach it. It remains trapped at its current height, and thus, in its energy state. Science calls such a state metastable. In other words, temporarily stable. Water, in this case, forms a lake, a mountain pond, or an artificial reservoir. Or—on a smaller scale but for exactly the same reasons—even a puddle on an uneven road after rain."

The professor scanned the room, and since she didn't observe any bewildered expressions, she concluded that everything was clear for now.

"The reservoir may exist for many years, but we can all agree it's not eternal. A sudden cloudburst, surpassing engineering calculations, can quickly fill the structure, and the level exceeds the dam's capacity. The overflowing current initially carries small debris, but as the furrow deepens, larger and heavier pieces of material are swept away until the dam breaks. Nothing stops the water anymore from fulfilling the destiny dictated by the natural law of energy minimization. Without hesitation, it seizes the opportunity and rush with usually destructive impact down to lower levels. And here we come to the point," she continued, noting a slightly growing impatience in some faces.

"The vacuum has been in a metastable state throughout the entire existence of the universe—at the fundamental, but not the lowest energy level. More precisely, that was the case until recently."

Everyone listened intently, and as they began to anticipate where the professor was heading, no one really wanted to know what was to follow.

"All observed parameters suggest that at the location where the blue dwarf star recently existed, along with the *Eremus* spacecraft sent by humanity fifty-six years ago, an energetic impulse and a process occurred in which the metastable vacuum began to collapse into a lower-energy state. According to the opinion of several renowned scientists, this event, this breakthrough of the barrier, was caused by the *Eremus*'s propulsion, utilizing the Casimir effect, a theoretically known and later experimentally utilized phenomenon since the mid-twentieth century. However, precisely the fact that this propulsion has been in use for several decades goes against this claim.

"In the opinion of the second group of scientists, another unknown energetic event must have played a role here, causing the vacuum's transformation. The last signals received from *Eremus* suggest that the interaction between Tristan Smolensky and object on the surface of the asteroid orbiting the blue dwarf star could be that additional event. There might also be a possible connection to the appearance of the dwarf star itself in that region of spacetime. This could have influenced the stability of the vacuum or had an impact on the height of the energy barrier."

She noticed signs of confusion arising from the use of scientific terms, as well as the skeptical glances betraying doubts among some members of the highest military and security structures. Questions lingered: Did the military approve the use of these technologies? Were military experts involved in crew selection? These were undoubtedly thoughts crossing their minds at this moment.

"To defend our scientists, it's crucial to emphasize that such an event couldn't have been predicted in advance. Unfortunately, we lack knowledge about the nature or content of the object. Due to the limited speed of light and data processing, we're yet to uncover all the circumstances surrounding the interaction between *Eremus* and the object. What's crucial, however, is that the vacuum transformation brings about a complete change in the properties of spacetime and the structure of everything within it, including particles and, consequently, matter."

Once again, she had to swallow dryly and moisten her throat with another sip of water. The following sentences would not be easy to articulate.

"The transformation of vacuum into a state with lower energy will completely destroy all existing particles, atoms, molecules, stars, and galaxies. The universe will acquire unknown properties—perhaps with new particles, perhaps without them. The world as we know it will cease to exist."

This time, the cold glares in the room were replaced by determined frowning faces accompanied by the hum of starting discussions. In their minds, they evidently began to categorize the degree of threat and focus on selecting the most suitable scenarios for addressing this type of situation.

It was unlikely, though, that any suitable scenarios existed.

"Please, a moment of your attention again," she urged those present for the second time. She continued deliberately and slowly, articulating precisely to allow understanding of her words.

"According to our observations, the transformation or breakdown of the vacuum from the former dwarf star's location is spreading spherically in all directions at a speed reaching approximately 99.95 percent of the speed of light. Therefore, we know about it with a slight advance. We don't see the transformation of the vacuum itself; we see high-energy radiation generated by the decay of particles in the locations of the advancing front of vacuum transformation. This is what damaged our power and communication network. It's just a faint hint before the full 'transformational wave.'" The professor indicated the use of quotation marks with a gesture at the last phrase.

"The radiation is slightly, about one twentieth of percent, ahead of it. Given the distance from the former blue dwarf star, we have approximately a week until it reaches us."

The grave silence, now sounding unnatural and ominous, returned. Everyone probably slowly began to grasp the full meaning of the professor's announcement, but not enough to start asking questions.

The first to recover was a man in the front row dressed in a blue four-star military uniform. "Is there any method to reverse, halt, or at least decelerate this process, enabling a portion of humanity to evacuate Earth? Alternatively, is there a possibility of interpreting the data in a less catastrophic manner than currently presented?"

A surprisingly prompt and stoic reaction to the announcement of the world's demise, the professor thought approvingly.

"Unfortunately, the answer to both questions is no. The observed phenomena are of an extensive nature, spreading spherically in all directions and precisely corresponding to the calculations of vacuum decay. We are not aware of any possibilities our civilization could use to halt the process. On the contrary, from a physical standpoint, it is an unstoppable and unrelenting process that even the most advanced civilization could not reverse. And given the speed of propagation, which is close to the speed of light, escape is unrealistic."

Despite the extraordinary gravity of the topic and the multitude of people present, no one could muster another question at that moment. The information was either too shocking for complete comprehension, or it was enough to set in motion the procedural steps for dealing with a planet-wide catastrophe, with specific questions arising from experts later, during the implementation of these procedures.

It's paradoxical that what enabled our creation will also destroy us in a week, thought the professor, but she didn't deem it necessary to present this addition to the fate of humanity publicly[14]. As a scientist, she was accustomed to a significant mismatch between the volume and intensity of internal thoughts and the number of words presented to the external world. Therefore, with a sigh, she only concluded the thought internally: *After all, the previous vacuum decay, in the first fractions of a second after the creation of the universe, initially slowed down its drastic expansion, allowing everything we know today, including ourselves, to come into existence. Truly emblematic of the intricate interplay of cosmic forces...*

The professor calmly distanced herself from the lectern, leaving the room to the sounds of an awakening murmur. She was surprised that the impending cataclysm evoked barely any excitement or sorrow within her, only a humble acceptance of the natural laws. These laws didn't recognize the concepts of good and evil—such attributes were often unjustifiably ascribed by some arrogant creatures based solely on their subjective and egocentric consequences.

Natural laws permitted only one possibility: the necessary evolution and processes that occurred in accordance with them —in other words, a universal harmony, whether any clump of matter and energy liked it or not.

XXV – CANDIDATE

Earth, year 2062
The first RW chapter

Pitch-black darkness. Absolute nothingness and emptiness. And suddenly... a sharp flash, something like the rebirth of the universe. Maybe reliving visions, this time of the beginning of the universe, the Big Bang?

No, it wasn't absolute nothingness, because there he was, his entity, his ego. His own self.

And that was precisely the complication. How was it that only he was there? Where was... where was QuWa? How was it that he felt different than before?

An unknown male voice came from somewhere, sounding laconic and matter-of-fact. "It seems he is waking up."

Suddenly, he realized that the intense brightness was gradually fading, but it wasn't enough to recognize details of the surrounding environment. His senses were slowly, but surely, becoming aware of the abstract patterns swirling around him—or perhaps within him.

He tried to identify something specific, a hint, a focal point that would help him emerge from the uncertainty and ambiguity in which he groped like a novice navigating through a maze. However, he couldn't succeed. Every time he thought the abstract shapes were clustering into a more concrete form, they immediately dissolved again into an unreadable whirlwind of colors, patterns, and shapes.

"All right, administer the standard dose of adrenaline," another voice, this time higher, gentler, and sounding older, suddenly said. "Intravenously and slowly... Monitor blood pressure and heart rate during this."

He felt a surge of energy in his veins. Initially slow, it gradually intensified, penetrating to the marrow of his bones. Was it a genuine sensation originating from his veins and bones, or merely the electromagnetic equivalent of this feeling?

Before he could unravel the answers, the bizarre patterns shifted. Like the wind in the high mountains dispersing thick fog that obscures the surroundings, the patterns seemed to have been startled by something, and they nervously accelerated their chaotic dance. They gradually began to fade, losing the vividness and intensity of colors.

"Try to open your eyes," he heard someone say after a while.

Who should do so? After all, he saw no one... and, by the way, what eyes?

Then, he realized it.

He had his eyes closed! The swirling colors had completely prevented him from realizing that his lids were shut. Suddenly, he experienced the familiar sensation of a banal situation when waking up. How was it possible that it seemed to him that he had eyes? Was it just the equivalent of old sensations, something like phantom feelings known from surgery, where individuals continued to perceive an amputated limb even though they no longer had it physically? After all, after merging with QuWa, he no longer had any eyes!

Nevertheless, he concentrated and invested all his energy into the effort to open his lids partially. Nothing. No response. It was as if he were trying to lift the thousand-year-old trunk of a mighty Californian sequoia with his bare hands—a futile effort. Surely, it was just a phantom sensation. He had nothing to open. Yet, instead of relief, he paradoxically began to feel uneasy, bound, as if in captivity.

"You can speed up the adrenaline injection; the electroencephalogram indicates that brain activity is slightly ahead of the course of the physical reaction," the higher of the two voices gently announced.

He felt another surge of energy, and suddenly, it was here. A thin, shimmering streak cut through the darkness like a crack in the night sky. After a moment of stagnation, it began to widen imperceptibly and thicken. A fissure to another world—that was how he perceived it. Under the pressure of the blinding light, which spurted from it like propellants from a rocket engine, he reflexively had to slacken his efforts.

The fissure diminished slightly, but did not disappear. After a moment, he mustered the courage to resist the flood of light and focused his effort on his eyelids once again. This time, the radiant stream was somewhat weaker. Consequently, he could open what he felt as his eyes a bit more without pain. The crack turned into a wide rift, gradually occupying a larger part of his field of vision, until it became a broad arc. Within it, he began to perceive growing irregularities, darker and lighter spots, and even hints of colors.

Finally! He succeeded in identifying the first enduring shape lasting longer than a second. At least, his mind perceived the time interval as a second.

It looked like a tall building, or perhaps a crane with its arm extended over his face. Or maybe... he scrutinized it more closely, trying to focus his vision and capture as many details as possible. He could see better now; the image sharpened, gaining more detailed contours.

What he saw startled him. If he correctly interpreted the image received by his detection system—whatever it might be—a biomedical unit was leaning over him. He was convinced by the view on the right and by the effort to move his right hand. His eyes could see that an intravenous catheter was attached to his hand—a tube through which some liquid flowed slowly, drop by drop. And he couldn't move the hand because it was tethered to the bed with a black strap.

What did this mean? Where was this? How was it that he had his physical body again? Had there been a malfunction or a reverse rejection of the connection with QuWa, a failure in the transformation into a photon-based life form?

"Welcome back, Tristan." The gentle female voice that he could now match visually interrupted the growing confusion. It belonged to an older woman wearing a white coat, along with a plastic head cover bordered by a flexible edge, reminiscent of the hygiene gear worn by doctors during surgeries. She had a white mask over her mouth, slightly muffling and blurring her precise articulation.

"Don't worry, everything is fine; you'll be as good as new shortly."

That's easy for you to say. How am I supposed not to worry when I don't understand what's happening to me and where I am? he wondered as his futile attempt to produce a sound resembling these words resulted only in a brief rasp. Without embarrassment, it would have created a fitting sound backdrop for a horror movie about a monster emerging from a mysterious tangle and opening its jaws covered in dripping slime.

"Fifty centiliters of water. Orally," said the woman, as if solely for recording purposes, and placed a tube with clear liquid to his lips.

Never would he have imagined that ordinary water could taste so delectable, so divinely invigorating. It was scintillatingly refreshing and soothingly reminiscent of chamomile balm. His desiccated throat welcomed those fifty centiliters, those few sips, more than if they had presented him with the sweetest liquid elixir.

The effect manifested swiftly. "Where am I?" he managed to rasp out.

"As I said, don't worry. Everything is fine. You find yourself in the *Enpeecee*, specifically in the active sector," the woman responded calmly. "I apologize; I haven't introduced myself yet. I am Dr. Zachary, the chief specialist in returns."

"What... what is this *Enpeecee*? And... a specialist in returns from where?" he managed to articulate under the onslaught of uncertainties, aided by the fact that adrenaline was starting to have a better effect, and water was lubricating his vocal cords.

"Ah, I see you're still disoriented," replied the doctor in a tone carrying a blend of understanding and instructiveness, somewhat like when parents addressed children in situations where they didn't comprehend their surroundings. "That's okay; don't worry. It's understandable. No one has gone as far as you have yet."

At that moment, clarity began to dawn. Memory neurons started communicating with the rest of the brain. And he didn't like what they were telling him. *Enpeecee... Enpeecee... neonatal prevention center. No, no, that couldn't be the right association. Try again.*

Ah, NPC... He finally recalled the abbreviated form for Neurosimulation Pre-flight Center. Its goal was to test the psychological resilience, predispositions, and personality integrity of candidates.

No, this must be just an unpleasant dream—some memory of the past with a physical body. Surely, he would wake up in the comforting embrace of his new photon existence any moment now.

However, nothing like that happened. He closed his eyes, ignoring the doctor's voice.

No, this was not what he desired. He didn't wish for this even in his worst nightmare. After experiencing the beauty of photon existence, he didn't want to go back. He couldn't go back. Evolution was not reversible; it could only move forward, not backtrack. Perhaps these horrors haunting him would disappear shortly.

It surprised him that even in the photon stage of evolution, there were dreams or visions, even unpleasant ones. He felt a bit resentful towards QuWa for not warning him, not preparing him in advance.

Well, he'd wait; everything had its end. Even this dream must come to an end.

***

Even after a considerable amount of time had passed since his futile attempt to bury his head in the sand, nothing had changed. More precisely, something had changed—his senses were much sharper, his perception clearer, his memories more complex, and... his self-awareness more tormenting. He still lay on the same bed, perceiving the same surroundings, but this time, in greater detail.

At that moment, the woman—what was her name? Sakari, or something like that—entered the room. "So, feeling better now?" she asked with a soft, optimistic voice.

"No," he replied succinctly but accurately.

"I understand. Allow me to clarify your situation for you, just to be sure."

Finally. Perhaps now, he would hear some nonsense, something inconsistent that would reassure him that it was just a dream.

"Firstly, this is neither a dream nor a vision." The doctor froze his hope as if she could read his thoughts.

Indeed, it's a stubborn vision, he reluctantly thought to himself.

"I'm sure you recall that before your launch, you underwent psychological and neurophysiological tests to verify your ability to undertake a challenging expedition to the blue dwarf—"

"Of course I remember!" Tristan didn't let the doctor finish. "Everything went well, and I launched as the most suitable candidate."

"Not quite," the doctor continued. "Neurotests and neurosimulations were highly complex. Such an exceptional expedition required exceptional candidates, hence an exceptional selection and choice."

"Of course," Tristan responded without hesitation, "and what do you mean by saying I wasn't quite a suitable candidate? Is this some new form of communication? Are you some autonomous communication software? I haven't communicated with anyone for decades, except for Aurora recently—well, actually, except for the onboard AI—and I'll never communicate face-to-face like this again over a distance of forty light-years."

"You are mistaken," the doctor answered patiently. "You are not, and you have never been forty light-years away from Earth. You have been and still are on our planet. Only two hours and forty-two minutes have passed since the beginning of the simulation."

An unpleasant sensation began to grip him.

"The task of neurosimulation tests was to verify your reactions to various situations, complications, or problems that might arise. At the same time, they aimed to test your determination, stability, and reliability during a long journey."

It was no longer just an unpleasant feeling. It was dreadful. His stomach was beginning to feel intensely constricted.

"The fundamental parameters of the simulation were externally introduced, particularly the altered neurotransmitter levels. However, most other attributes and situations, such as the specific form of the extraterrestrial civilization, were generated by your own mind and personality traits. As mentioned, the goal was to test you in boundary and non-standard conditions. Before entering the simulation, you agreed to and signed relevant declarations."

"But..." He gasped for breath, vaguely recalling reminiscences of past events, buried in the whirlwind of recent intense experiences. "That... that can't be possible! Now, I am aware of not only my own thoughts but, out of nowhere, also moments I never witnessed firsthand. Records of press conferences and the thoughts of my friends! QuWa's thoughts too! And the destruction of Earth? That doesn't make any sense! I... I remember now that I actually died before that, shortly after the transformation!"

"The realization and perception of these facts should convince you that it wasn't reality. How else could you learn about them in such detail and broad perspective? Neurosimulation is a complex and sophisticated process that cannot provide realistic results without globally covering all branches of the situation's development. Everything is interconnected, like the cogs of a machine.

"You primarily perceived what directly concerned you, but the simulation was much more robust, including its proper completion after your death. It has capabilities beyond simple replication of experiences. It's the first step in creating a form of collective consciousness and memory sharing. It's the pride of our research center—our contribution to the evolution of humankind. Upon the simulation's conclusion, a part of the parallel events infiltrated your consciousness and integrated into the correct temporal context to prevent any disruption of causality that might endanger your mental well-being. This is a well-known and non-threatening side effect."

He was losing solid ground beneath his feet—or, rather, the resilient bed beneath him. The world began to spin around him.

"My mental health is more endangered by that simulated death and this dramatic revelation than some causality... So, all those events passed only in my mind?" he asked in disbelief, shaken and resigned.

"Yes. The analysis of the simulation's progress is not complete yet, but don't worry—you will receive the results in the coming days."

The stomach-churning evolved into a chilling sensation, and its nearly empty contents, consisting mainly of hydrochloric acid and other digestive juices, controlled by the vomiting reflex evolved for cases of poisoning, pushed upward against his constricted esophagus.

***

A sound signal indicated the reception of the long-awaited message. After an imperceptibly short moment needed for identity verification and decryption, the ominously anticipated result appeared before his eyes.

Subject #297, neurosimulation #297/058.
Result: failure.
Justification: egotistic prioritization of personal progress over the interest of the civilization, irresponsible attempt to contact the originator of the anomaly without sufficient prior analysis...

His vision blurred. He couldn't read any further.

Alone. Never before had this feeling penetrated his thoughts so deeply, seizing them with unwavering force, momentarily eclipsing all else—akin to a supernova outshining its galaxy with a flood of photons and neutrinos.

Alone with his thoughts. He could only blame himself.

Would there be another attempt? Would he ever be capable of undertaking it anymore?

***

After months of testing, simulations, analyses, and evaluations, the scientists had finally managed to select the most suitable candidate. A success rate of 99.3 percent—the best that humanity could offer.

Everything was ready for launch.

XXVI – ALONE (EPILOGUE)

Eremus *spaceship, year 2120*
The second RW (real world) chapter

Silence. If there were an alert creature here, it would say the silence was almost deafening. However, no such creature was on board, only a human in cryosleep. Yet the ship's system was vigilant. Thanks to the significantly shorter distance, it received and analyzed signals originating from the destination in much greater detail than was possible when the signals had been analyzed on Earth from forty light-years distance. Recently, it had detected entirely new faint frequencies—ones that even the most powerful telescopes and detectors on Earth hadn't captured.

Suddenly, in the middle of the room, like embers in a primeval cave lit by shimmering flames, tiny lights flickered. It wasn't a fire—in a subdued glow, colorful illuminated lines danced on the holopanel, even though there was no one to see them. The ship's reactor fueled powerful processing cores that tirelessly, for almost thirty-five years, had been deciphering signals from the destination that had remained incomprehensible until now. Thirty-five years, petabytes of data, and no success, just like on Earth.

Until now.

The cryogenic pod slowly began to brighten and change color, transitioning from a faintly subdued red, indicating full sleep mode, to a slightly more pronounced pale blue. The awakening sequence had started. That was the good news.

Less pleasing, however, was the fact that the sequence, according to the standard mission schedule, was supposed to be initiated in approximately six months.

The bright hues on the holopanel faded abruptly, and the vivid lines ceased dancing, with only the partially decrypted text subtly and statically glowing.

> *Caution.*
> *...[undeciphered]... Upon arrival,*
> *Eschew void propulsion...[undeciphered]...*
> *Peril of void collapse.*
> *Alternatives ...[undeciphered]... presented.*
> *Anticipate ...[undeciphered]... further communication.*

Author's note:

Dear Readers,

As we reach the conclusion of this journey, I wanted to offer an opportunity for reflection and choice. The primary ending of the story invites you into a realm that questions reality, embracing the thought-provoking and often ambiguous nature of open endings. This approach may resonate with those who appreciate works where the boundaries of perception and existence are constantly explored.

In recognition of the diverse tastes within the science fiction community, I have also prepared an alternative ending, grounded in the principles of hard science fiction. This approach adheres more closely to the *many-worlds interpretation of quantum mechanics* and is designed to appeal to readers who prefer a narrative that aligns more with scientific rigor and logical consistency.

Both endings emerge from the same narrative foundation, yet they diverge to cater to different reader preferences. The alternative ending follows immediately **after Chapter XXIV, "Metastability"**, providing a distinct path where no neuro-simulation or awakening of a failed candidate occurs.

I invite you to choose the ending that aligns best with your tastes, expectations, and preferences, allowing you to experience the story in a way that is most fulfilling for you.

Thank you for joining me on this journey.

ALTERNATIVE ENDING

ALTEND XXV – BACK

Blue dwarf system, year 2121

He still couldn't believe it. The transformation had been successful.

Accomplishment filled him to the brim, like a jug at the well of knowledge. Skipping over eons of evolutionary progress, he now had permanent and inseparable access to the tremendous knowledge and abilities of a civilization that had survived epochs of time. Although originating from another universe, it shared enough similarities that its insights could almost fully apply to ours.

Realizing he was connected to QuWa, as if tethered by an umbilical cord, he felt both himself and yet intertwined to the core with something resembling a cloud or a soup, where boundaries between him and others dissolved. There were also empty areas, resembling deserts, where semi-autonomous entities like him existed but had been damaged or destroyed during the unintended transfer to our high-energy universe.

He no longer had a physical body. A strange state. His mind had not yet fully adapted to the bizarre perception of being bodiless; he still tended to feel it somehow. But it was temporary. QuWa's experience indicated that phantom feelings would quickly fade, and the merging would be completed even on a mental level.

It was incredibly beautiful. He no longer needed those very unpleasant metal cans for space travel. He was as free as a bird, or rather, many times freer than that bird in the sky. He could travel as a wave packet wherever he wanted, spreading as pure photon waves with minimal energy wherever he pleased.

And the most exciting part was that he could do it *instantly*. Traveling at the speed of light meant that time locally stopped for him during the transfer. Breathtaking. To whatever place he desired to go, he could get there in no time for him[15]. Absolute freedom, the shackles of space and time were gone.

Of course, in the surrounding universe, time still flowed, so the journey to Earth, which they decided to undertake as QuWa, would take forty years from the perspective of an Earthling. But for him, it would be just an eyeblink. Or more precisely, a *photon-blink*. He immensely enjoyed this freedom, this huge leap in possibilities.

He even relinquished his original resolution to have nothing to do with humanity anymore. Perhaps it was a side effect of the transformation. In the end, the feeling of kinship prevailed, and after having experienced the freedom and openness of this new form of existence, he couldn't help but bring this news, this gift, to his fellow Earthlings.

However, the feeling of fulfillment was hindered by something. Metastability. Metastability troubled him. He realized that the conference announcing the cataclysm had been an illusion, a vision, vividly experienced as an alternative, a warning from QuWa about a possibility that could have happened but fortunately did not. At least not yet. The vacuum drive was not a good path. He had deeply felt and knew that it was a risky propulsion method that threatened this entire universe.

It was astonishing that in our universe, a civilization had not yet developed to use it and cause this catastrophic collapse. Or maybe it had developed but had reached a similar conclusion as QuWa and abandoned the technology as dangerous before a statistically probable collapse occurred. Or perhaps there was a slight difference in the physical properties of particles in our universe, making the risk of vacuum collapse somewhat less likely.

But it was definitely not responsible to test it. Experimental measurements would surely continue under strict control, but the conclusion was already clear—no to the vacuum drive. That's also why he had to return. To warn. Because otherwise, QuWa could be destroyed, and he indubitably could not let that happen.

However, this was just the beginning. The knowledge of QuWa was enormous, but there will always be endless treasures yet to uncover.

The truly exciting, the real leap forward, awaited around the corner.

First of all, though, he now faced the journey back, the return to the planet he had been convinced he would never see again—the return to Earth.

ALTEND XXVI – MIGRATION

Earth, year 2166 (40 years of travel back and five years after arrival)

"Slowly and one at a time!" commanded the strict, ringing voice of the operating personnel. "Do not worry, there will be ample opportunity for everyone."

The Photon Migration Center, built in record time, was bursting at the seams. The transformation technology provided by QuWa was an immense success, and hundreds of millions of people voluntarily chose to undergo the transformation into photon form of existence. Initially, there were intense discussions about whether anyone could undergo it or if it was limited to selected advanced individuals. Wouldn't people carry their personality traits, with all their negatives, into the photon form of existence? Would it not just be *Humanity 2*, with all the flaws it possesses? Wars, egoism, disdain for others—the list of negative traits or personality characteristics could fill an entire book. Would individuals not carry them into the new form of existence, gaining only greater power and technological means to achieve their petty goals? Isn't humanity simply too immature?

The QuWa had provided the answer right from the start—the transformation did not mean copying the original individual. Hundreds of billions of years at their disposal had allowed them to optimize the technology and process to such an extent that any elements threatening civilization as a whole had been filtered out during the migration. It was like a thorough cleansing of the individual from all the deposits that would hinder common existence. To many, it seemed almost mystical, unreal, reminiscent of entering paradise—all negatives erased, forgotten, only positive traits remained. A purgatory based on physics. From a logical perspective, however, it was nothing extraordinary or unexpected—it was purely a matter of compatibility, as if the code of the human mind was rid of errors and sources of inconsistency, and after cleansing, merged into the cloud of QuWa semi-autonomous entities. Programmers would call it debugging.

So, there were no conditions for the transformation. More precisely, there was only one—the willingness to undergo it.

Despite scheduling a specific appointment, queues still formed. Modern technology did not automatically mean complete adherence to the schedule, as it could not influence human errors and shortcomings such as delays, hold-ups during necessary administrative steps, or hesitation at the last moments. In any case, excitement and general enthusiasm prevailed in the queue.

Suddenly, there was a deafening roar.

"Boom!"

It was not a launch of a spaceship. A massive explosion shook the vestibule of the migration center.

"Disperse! Disperse!" someone shouted, trying to overpower the cacophony that immediately filled the surroundings after the explosion.

"Here, here please!" another voice desperately called from elsewhere, trying to summon help for the injured.

"Doctor, doctor, quickly!"

A mix of shouts, pleas, and alarming tones blended into one urgent buzz, like when a hive of bees is disturbed by an unexpected intruder.

No wonder. By far, not everyone was interested in the transformation. Some feared losing their identity, others preferred our world over an unknown one without tangible guarantees. Resistance movements even emerged, alarming people that it was actually hostile assimilation aiming to erase humanity from the Earth's surface after completion. A typical human trait—fear of the unknown, fear of the unfamiliar and foreign.

Some resistance movements, however, did not stop at mere agitation. Unfortunately, even the strictest security measures could not prevent an accident and the misfortune of a terrorist attack.

Humanity was very fortunate to have encountered a civilization that had long ago discovered that from an evolutionary perspective, it was more beneficial to build together than to destroy. Naive pacifism? Wars and violence have historically spurred humanity to make revolutionary progress; for instance, the technological boom brought about by World War II is a notable example. Jet propulsion, rocket engines, encryption of data... none of this would have developed so quickly without the war frenzy and the effort to outdo the enemy at all costs, regardless of resources. Peace does not create such intense pressure for advancement because there is no enemy to be urgently and swiftly surpassed.

However, from a global perspective, peaceful development is more advantageous; it provides sometimes slower but more sustainable growth that is not only morally cleaner but above all more resource-efficient, as it thinks economically rather than politically or militarily. An impressive example is SpaceX's conquest of the Moon and Mars during the first half of the 21st century. No, war efforts and political hostility ultimately do not advance civilization as much as the peaceful concentration of resources and efforts based on pragmatism rather than feverish striving.

Nevertheless, not everyone shared this principle. The explosion confirmed this. The naive pacifist approach received a harsh lesson, a cold shower of real life. But nothing will stop the evolution of humankind. And it clearly headed towards photon existence. Regardless of local resistance, globally, most of humanity would undergo transformation, seen by many as an entry into paradise. Atheists viewed it as a Darwinian victory, the final phase of evolution; religiously inclined people saw it as approaching God or gods, as a gift from heaven in the form of universal mutual love, reconciliation, respect, and harmony that God brought through QuWa. Justified in every way, hundreds of millions of people underwent transformation in thousands of centers built solely for this purpose.

Humankind is opening up new horizons. Traveling in zero time for the crew of a massless cosmic ship is one of them. Ah, what a dream for every inquisitive soul.

ALTEND XXVII – ANOTHER

499 light-years from Earth, year 2660 Earth Time

"Requesting status analysis," Tristan prompted by train of thought. It felt strange to communicate solely through thoughts. Though nearly half a millennium had passed on Earth, for him, it had been relatively little time to fully adapt. Yes, traveling at the speed of light allowed one to traverse vast distances practically in an instant, as time froze within the explorer's environment. Distances no longer mattered; the universe had "shrunk" far more than Earth had after the advent of mass air travel in the twentieth century.

Tristan had not yet accustomed himself to this new form of existence. They were the first photon-based expedition to delve into the depths of our universe, pioneers of its exploration. Such voyages were the only exceptions for the brave, temporarily separating them from the rest of civilization. They no longer needed to search for a new Earth; the issue of overpopulation was automatically resolved by transformation. Photon existence required no food; solar energy sufficed, abundant enough at this stage of development, nor did it require as much space or orbital structures as physical bodies[16].

However, they did require knowledge, information, understanding—attributes befitting an advanced civilization. This universe was new to QuWa. Despite mastering the deformation of spacetime that brought QuWa into our universe, it wasn't a process they could utilize for routine travel. Firstly, the required energy was enormous, and secondly, it involved highly risky and unstable processes. After all, their unexpected shift into our universe confirmed this. It wasn't unlike the situation in the mid-twentieth century when humanity was enthusiastic and optimistic about technological progress. But in reality, technological progress was much more modest and restrained. Similarly, physical laws and energy constraints limited the possibilities of travel even for an advanced civilization like QuWa. Wormhole travel simply wasn't on the agenda, remaining beyond the reach of routine travel. Not to mention that traveling at the speed of light was, after all—amazing.

"All systems are nominal. No deviations from expected values," Johan, originally a pilot in material life, replied.

He was among the first individuals to undergo transformation and join Tristan as soon as it was feasible. They embarked on their exploratory journey as a team of ten—the most skilled individuals with a sincere and intense desire for cosmic knowledge. Solitary flights were prohibited due to the QuWa's semi-autonomous nature; being alone was deemed unnatural and perilous.

However, traveling at the speed of light meant interacting with particles of the surrounding universe—and photons were no exception. Hence, they had to adhere to physical laws like any other elementary particle—preparing photon shields to deflect unwanted interactions with interstellar matter and photons from stars and relic cosmic radiation.

This was no easy task. Each atom of interstellar gas, each relic photon from the early universe posed a potential collision hazard during light-speed travel. The photon shield eliminated these collisions, although its lifespan was not unlimited—it formed at the start of the journey and gradually wore down and weakened with collisions with particles. Renewing it during the journey was very inefficient without material equipment. And zero rest mass was, after all, the basis of travel.

Nevertheless, the likelihood of shield collisions with

particles was not excessively high, so journeys were limited to an impressive action radius of thousands of light-years. What would people sacrifice to be able to travel such distances? Many would give their lives for it. And now it's here.

It usually wasn't possible to slow down at the destination, they could only come to a complete halt. QuWa could exist either as a wave packet moving at the speed of light in vacuum or as stationary wave which depended on the destination, moving very slowly compared to the speed of light. The limits of physical laws are relentless. To stop and transform from wave packets back into standing waves required extremely precise coordination with the radiation of the target star and the surrounding plasma. Stopping at the destination was one of the great achievements of the QuWa, developed in their ancient times when there was still matter present. Later, they adapted it to universe devoid of mass particles, relying solely on relic radiation. However, utilizing stars proved more efficient and reliable, though not all destinations were suitable for such a maneuver.

Moreover, traveling at the speed of light meant there was no time "during" the flight, requiring them to prepare the next stop beforehand. Therefore, they proceeded with small steps: from star to a close star; a hop, measurement, and preparation for the next hop. This starhopping technique ensured minimal unexpected surprises. Thus, the smaller the steps, the higher the probability of success and safety. QuWa had mastered this technique well already in ancient times, but this was their first time employing it in our universe.

By this approach, it was of course also possible to return to Earth. However, no one was currently considering a return to their home planet—the present offered a fascinating object of study, the star they had discovered during the latest stop of this exploratory journey.

"The spectrum shows a peak in energies corresponding to the blue region of the visible spectrum," Johan said.

"That's impossible! Unless we made an error in calculating

the mass!" Tristan responded incredulously.

"An error is out of the question. The accuracy of the calculation is high, with a margin of error no greater than one percent. Based on the orbital period of the planet around the star, it is clear that the star's mass is only one-tenth that of the Sun... But... Do you know what that means, my friends?"

"I can't believe it! Improbable! That is... that's another *blue dwarf*! QuWa might have company!"

Your Thoughts Matter

Dear Reader,

Thank you so much for journeying through the pages of *Blue Anomaly*. I hope you found the adventure both enriching and engaging. I devoted many hundreds of hours and countless sleepless nights to showcase the beauty of the universe. My goal was to popularize science and instill a sense of wonder about our world and the laws of nature in an entertaining way—the same wonder I feel when looking up at the stars.

Your thoughts and reflections are incredibly valuable to me. If you enjoyed exploring the universe with Tristan, it would mean the world to me if you could take a few moments to share your review on Amazon and/or Goodreads. Your feedback not only helps me grow as an author, but also aids fellow readers in discovering new tales that might resonate with them.

Thank you for your support and for being a vital part of this journey.

Wishing you many delightful reads,

J.K. Bunta

APPENDIX A: SCIENTIFIC FOUNDATIONS OF THE STORY

i) StarTram

An electromagnetic method of transportation to orbit through a vacuum tunnel, exiting at high altitudes in mountainous regions, is a well-developed concept closely aligned with current technological possibilities.

ii) Dynamical Casimir Effect

The dynamical Casimir effect is a physical phenomenon bringing a potential prospect of dramatic reduction of the mass of a spacecraft. Theoretical predictions were made in the 1970s, and its first experimental confirmation was published in 2011, when scientists managed to create microwave photons from a vacuum.

The occurrence stems from the so-called static Casimir effect, theoretically predicted by Dutch physicist Hendrik Casimir in 1947 after consultations with Nobel laureate Niels Bohr, and experimentally confirmed in 1997. This effect occurs when two parallel plates are brought close enough, leading to a reduction in the production of virtual particles between them from a quantum physics perspective. As a result, a region with energy lower than the vacuum energy (which is not zero, according to quantum theory) is created between the plates, causing a force and pressure attempting to bring the plates closer. Experimentally measured values correspond to theoretically calculated ones.

There is also a competing theoretical explanation for the existence of this force through relativistic Van der Waals forces. Determining which theoretical explanation of the observed Casimir force is correct remains a subject of further scientific investigation.

The static Casimir effect allows, among others, the creation of a rechargeable battery. However, for commercial use, a suitable shape and non-trivial geometry are required to ensure sufficient energy density.

iii) Aneutronic fusion

The aneutronic, i.e., neutronless fusion, is a fusion reaction that has been theoretically well-described and experimentally reliably demonstrated. It offers the advantage of minimal radiation, direct energy conversion, and thus high efficiency, safety, and environmental friendliness. Several technological approaches are currently under development with the goal of scaling up to commercial feasibility.

iv) Laser Nanosails

Laser-propelled nanocrafts, minuscule solar sails weighing only a few grams, accelerated by an Earth-based laser to speeds up to twenty percent of the speed of light in a short period, represent a well-founded concept. The implementation of this idea is underway through Breakthrough Starshot, a private project.

v) Blue Dwarf

The blue dwarf represents the final stage in low-mass star development, a phenomenon yet to be observed due to the young age of the universe. This stage was first theoretically predicted in 2005.

vi) Heat Death of the Universe

A heat death is a state where all transformation and energy transfer ceases, an inevitable outcome in an open universe, i.e., a universe where expansion continues indefinitely. Current astrophysical observations suggest that our universe is open.

vii) Photonic Molecule

A photon molecule is a theoretical concept wherein electromagnetic waves create structures with properties akin to molecular structures, but with broader possibilities and lower energy requirements.

viii) Metastable Vacuum Decay

The transition of the vacuum to a state with lower energy is a well-established theoretical property rooted in its quantum-mechanical nature. Rigorous theoretical calculations allow for experimental verification, particularly through examination of the mass ratio of the top quark and the Higgs boson. Recent data from the Large Hadron Collider at CERN suggests that our universe may currently be in a temporarily stable state, with the potential for such a transition.

It's plausible that such a transition occurred in the past, marking the end of the initial phase of rapid inflation after the Big Bang and shaping the universe's current natural laws and constants. However, as mentioned above, our vacuum might not have reached its ultimate lowest energy state yet.

ix) Parallel Universe Hypothesis

The hypothesis of parallel universes, also known as the multiverse hypothesis, postulates the existence of a large number of independent and rarely interacting universes.

Scientists search for traces of such collisions of our cosmos with others in the cosmic microwave background radiation. With enough energy, according to quantum theory and the general theory of relativity, it is possible to deform the spacetime of the parent universe to such an extent that the deformation separates like a bubble, creating a new independent universe with partially different properties and physical laws. If this hypothesis is correct, there would even be a natural selection, with universes conducive to creating daughter universes being more numerous.

The hypothesis also provides an answer to the pressing question of how our world has precisely the physical properties that allow the emergence of life. The explanation is that among many parallel universes, only those suitable for intelligent life would harbor beings asking such questions. This is known as the anthropic principle.

Among the proponents of the hypothesis of parallel universes, we find prominent figures in cosmology and astrophysics, such as Stephen Hawking, Alan Guth, Andrei Linde, Brian Greene, and Michio Kaku.

x) Neurotransmitters

The description in the story accurately reflects reality. Neurotransmitters play a fundamental role in shaping our perception, thinking, behavior, and overall worldview. Fluctuations in their levels have a crucial impact on neural (synaptic) connections and changes in mood, personality traits, and human behavior.

Furthermore, external molecules like LSD or psilocybin, which share a similar structure with natural neurotransmitters, bind to the same receptors in our brain. This can lead to various effects, including hallucinations and significant impacts on the psyche.

xi) Calculations of Event Dates

The dates of events were calculated in accordance with time dilation defined by the Special Theory of Relativity. The calculation involved constant acceleration, equivalent to one-tenth of Earth's gravitational acceleration during the first half of the journey, and equally intense deceleration with navigation to the orbit upon reaching the target star system, which is forty light-years away from the launch site.

APPENDIX B: ADDITIONAL SCIENTIFIC FACTS

i) **Interstellar Dust and Gas**

Particles of dust and gas pose a significant challenge for any interstellar journey. At relativistic speeds, even tiny microparticles and hydrogen atoms bombard the spacecraft similarly to particles in accelerators, causing intense radiation and material wear. Fortunately, measurements indicate that the Sun is located in a region of the galaxy with a low density of gas and dust, formed by supernova explosions several million years ago.

Highly durable and lightweight alloys, such as beryllium copper, as well as carbon aerogels, already exist and have demonstrated self-healing capabilities in experiments. Properly arranged layers of these materials in the direction of travel can effectively protect the spacecraft.

Moreover, with acceleration corresponding to only one-tenth of Earth's gravitational acceleration, the ship reaches a maximum speed of 95 percent of the speed of light at the midpoint of the journey. This reduces particle energy compared to acceleration generating the equivalent of Earth's gravity, further improving the efficiency of the vessel's protection.

ii) **Radiation Shielding**

The level of radiation generated by collisions of a spacecraft with interstellar particles and cosmic radiation at relativistic speeds is extreme. However, it can be reduced through multilayered protection. A magnetic shield placed in front of the ship effectively blocks charged particles. The portion that penetrates it (such as neutral particles or gamma radiation), along with secondary radiation produced by particle absorption in the protective layers, can be mitigated by a combination of layers made of materials that absorb various types and energies of particles.

In addition to conventionally known materials with a high density of protons and neutrons, experiments have revealed unconventional shielding possibilities using so-called radiovorous fungi. These fungi can convert a portion of radioactive gamma radiation into chemical energy, utilizing it for their growth and biomass formation, similar to how standard plants convert solar energy through photosynthesis.

Observations from the Chernobyl nuclear power plant after its accident, as well as experiments on the International Space Station, have shown that due to this radio-synthesis, fungi of the species *Cryptococcus neoformans*, *Wangiella dermatitidis*, and *Cladosporium sphaerospermum* in an environment with radiation up to five times normal values grow three times faster than in a regular environment. Radiovorous fungi can thus form a lightweight, self-growing, and self-repairing barrier, as they are undemanding in terms of nutrition.

iii) Curiosities of Evolution

Throughout hundreds of millions of years, Earth's nature has repeatedly arrived at organisms that are morphologically or functionally similar, despite lacking evolutionary relatedness. Notable examples include hydrodynamic adaptations for fast swimming and pursuing prey in fish (sharks), reptiles (ichthyosaurs, now extinct), and mammals (dolphins), all of them sharing almost identical overall shape. Similarly, there's convergent evolution seen in the development of wings in pterosaurs and bats, as well as the remarkably similar eye structures in humans and octopuses.

In contrast, paleontological records reveal instances of complete abandonment of certain body concepts, as seen in the Ediacaran fauna. This early attempt by Earth's nature to create multicellular organisms likely went extinct without leaving evolutionary descendants. Some members of this fauna grew to sizes of approximately one meter and, from today's perspective, appear as creatures from another planet.

iv) Intuition in Exact Science

Contrary to common belief that intuition has no place in exact science, history reveals the opposite. In ancient times, precise mathematical formulas, like the one calculating the volume of a truncated pyramid (Problem 14 on the Moscow Mathematical Papyrus), were discovered by the Ancient Egyptians without exact derivations or empirical experiments. Such precision couldn't be achieved through trials with vessels filled with sand or water, nor without the use of integral calculus, which wasn't discovered until three and a half millennia later.

Another notable example is Schrödinger's equation, the foundation of quantum mechanics, initially conceived intuitively by its creator Erwin Schrödinger (1887 – 1961) and later mathematically derived.

Henri Poincaré (1854 – 1912), the renowned French mathematician and theoretical physicist who laid the groundwork for the special theory of relativity and predicted the existence of gravitational waves as early as 1905, aptly summarized this fascinating ability: "We prove by logic, but we discover by intuition."

v) Why Plants Aren't Black

In Chapter I, the fascinating question of why plants are not black is posed. Considering black's maximum radiation energy absorption—a hallmark of efficiency in nature—this question is indeed logical. However, several factors prevent nature from adopting this seemingly optimal strategy:

- **Evolutionary Progress:** Evolution is an ongoing process, indicating that plants' coloration might evolve toward greater efficiency in the future. Furthermore, just as plants have historically been able to, animals might also be capable of photosynthesis in the not-too-distant future. An illustrative example is the green "solar-powered sea slug," *Elysia chlorotica*, which already possesses genes that support the endosymbiotic integration of photosynthesizing chloroplasts directly within its cells.
- **Current Effectiveness:** The photosynthesis mechanisms in place, primarily utilizing green chlorophyll, are already quite efficient, suggesting that the evolutionary pressure for a drastic change in pigment coloration may not be significant.
- **Innovative Pigments:** The existence of unique photosensitive pigments, such as phycoerythrins, and the behavior of complementary chromatic adaptation in certain cyanobacteria—which alter their pigments and, consequently, their colors based on the ocean depth they inhabit—illustrate nature's experiments with optimizing light absorption.
- **Energy Management Challenges:** Achieving higher energy absorption efficiency necessitates mechanisms for shielding against excessive light and dissipating heat—a particular challenge for terrestrial plants. This is crucial for managing the heat generated from absorbing highly energetic blue photons.
- **Photosynthesis Bottlenecks:** Inefficiencies in the photosynthesis process, especially the slow and ineffective enzyme responsible for carbon fixation (the so-called RuBisCo enzyme), present significant limitations. Improving this

enzyme's efficiency is essential, as absorbing more energy would be futile if this step could not keep pace.

- Evolutionary History: The predominance of chlorophyll might be a legacy of ancient Earth conditions, dominated by purple photosynthetic organisms. This historical factor suggests that the green color of contemporary plants is an evolutionary adaptation to utilize the spectral energies not absorbed by these ancient organisms.

I would like to extend my heartfelt gratitude to my family for their enduring patience and empathetic support throughout the writing process.

My deepest appreciation is reserved for my beloved wife, Silvia, whose significant and creative contributions were vital to the story's content and narrative coherence. Her discerning insights and wise counsel were invaluable in refining this story to its ultimate form.

I must also express my sincere thanks to Oren Eades, whose meticulous attention to detail and expertise in language polished every sentence to a shine.

Collaborating with both of you has been a profoundly rewarding experience, and this book has greatly benefited from your contributions.

---

[1] The blue dwarf represents the actual final developmental stage for low-mass stars, a stage not yet observed due to the universe's young age. Further information can be found in Appendix A, section v).

[2] The described facts are part of the real concept of StarTram, which is close to the current technological capabilities.

[3] It concerns the so-called dynamical Casimir effect, whose first experimental confirmation was published in 2011, when scientists succeeded in creating microwave photons from vacuum. More information can be found in Appendix A, section ii).

[4] The neutronless fusion reactor is a realistic and promising concept that utilizes experimentally confirmed and theoretically well-founded fusion of proton with boron. More information can be found in Appendix A, section iii).

[5] The Static Casimir effect allows for several applications, including the creation of a rechargeable battery, among others.

[6] Particles of dust and gas represent a significant risk for interstellar travel. More information on this topic is included in Appendix B, section i).

[7] Biological shielding against radiation is enabled by so-called radiotrophic fungi discovered after the Chernobyl disaster, which can utilize part of the radiation as a source of energy for their growth. More information is included in Appendix B, section ii).

[8] Miniature laser-driven solar sails are a firmly established concept,

already pursued by the private initiative Breakthrough Starshot, initiated with the involvement of Stephen Hawking.

[9] The described evolution is a physically inevitable consequence of the so-called open universe, which is best aligned with current observations. The final stage of its development is the so-called heat death, when any energy circulation ceases.

[10] Among the proponents of the hypothesis of parallel universes, we find some of the most renowned names in cosmology and astrophysics, such as Stephen Hawking, Alan Guth, Andrei Linde, Brian Greene, and Michio Kaku. More information is available in Appendix A, section ix).

[11] Appendix B, section iii) briefly highlights some interesting aspects of the evolution of terrestrial nature.

[12] In the past, precise mathematical formulas, such as those for calculating the volume of a truncated pyramid by the Ancient Egyptians or Schrödinger's equation as the foundation of quantum mechanics, have been discovered without exact derivation or empirical experiments. Further description can be found in Appendix B, section iv).

[13] *The Gateless Gate*, also known as *Wumen-Kuan*, is a collection of Zen koans (rationally unsolvable problems) compiled by the Buddhist monk Wumen (1183-1260), which are intended to help readers change their approach to evaluating the world and understand the paradoxical nature of human thinking.

[14] From quantum theory, metastability emerges as a natural property of the current vacuum. The latest experimental data indicates that our universe is only in a temporarily stable state, and vacuum decay is highly probable. More information is included in Appendix A, section viii).

[15] According to the Special Theory of Relativity, for particles traveling at the speed of light, time in the system of such a particle (the so-called proper time) is stopped and does not pass. This is why a photon has an infinite range and can reach us even from the very edge of the universe, which is not possible for any other particle mediating one of the four fundamental physical forces of the universe.

[16] From a physics perspective, photons belong to the category of bosons, which can concentrate in virtually unlimited quantities at a single location, unlike the so-called fermions (such as protons, neutrons, and electrons, which make up our bodies).

There is only one corner of the universe you can be certain of improving, and that's your own self.

Aldous Huxley (1894 – 1963)

English writer, philosopher, and pioneer in psychedelic exploration

ABOUT THE AUTHOR

J. K. Bunta

Holding a Ph.D. in Nuclear Physics, J.K. Bunta is a voracious seeker of the universe's most elusive truths and mysteries. His research endeavors spanned the dense matter of neutron stars, the intricate ways radiation impacts human DNA, and the fields of nuclear astrophysics, biophysics, and biochemistry. Yet a fascination with realms beyond these—exploring how biochemistry shapes the human mind and how our perceptions construct the world around us—remains pivotal for him as well.

As a prolific writer of scientific popularization articles, he marries his extensive scientific knowledge with a boundless imagination, venturing into science fiction. He offers readers a unique blend of speculative fiction that is as intellectually stimulating as it is grounded in scientific reality. Prepare to embark on a journey through the wonders and what-ifs of science as told by a mind deeply entrenched in the quest for knowledge.

Printed in Great Britain
by Amazon